THE
FLOATPLANE
NOTEBOOKS

A Novel

CLYDE EDGERTON

With a New Introduction by the Author

The University of South Carolina Press

*Published in Cooperation with the Institute for
Southern Studies of the University of South Carolina*

New material © 2017 University of South Carolina

Cloth edition published by Algonquin Books
Paperback edition published by the University of South Carolina Press
Columbia, South Carolina 29208

www.sc.edu/uscpress

Manufactured in the United States of America

26 25 24 23 22 21 20 19 18 17
10 9 8 7 6 5 4 3 2 1

Library of Congress Cataloging-in-Publication Data
can be found at http://catalog.loc.gov/.

ISBN 978-1-61117-822-7 (paperback)

THE FLOATPLANE NOTEBOOKS

SOUTHERN REVIVAL SERIES
Robert H. Brinkmeyer, Jr., Series Editor

For Catherine

When I die, hallelujah, by and by,
I'll fly away

CONTENTS

SERIES EDITOR'S PREFACE

The Southern Revivals series brings important works of literature by contemporary southern writers back to print. All selections in the series have enjoyed critical and commercial success. By returning these works to general circulation, we hope to deepen readers' understandings of, and appreciations for, not only specific authors but also the flourishing southern literary landscape. Not too long ago, it was a fairly straightforward task to distinguish literature by southerners, as most of their works focused on easily recognizable "southern" themes, perspectives, and settings. Those days are long gone. Literature by southerners is now quite literally all over the map, extending its reach from the coast of South Carolina to the heart of West Africa, from the bayous of Louisiana to the rain forests of Brazil, from the mountains of East Tennessee and to the deserts of the Southwest. As our list of resurrected books grows, Southern Revivals will bring readers to many of these places, taking them on journeys into regions near and far away, journeys that attest to the astonishing diversity of contemporary southern culture.

Clyde Edgerton's *The Floatplane Notebooks* is a splendid addition to the series, standing alongside Edgerton's first novel *Raney,* which is being republished simultaneously in Southern Revivals. As Edgerton reveals in his introduction to this new edition, the origins of *The Floatplane Notebooks* stretch back to one of his earliest stories, though it would be many years before it evolved into its final form. As he also makes clear in his introduction, *The Floatplane Notebooks* is dear to Edgerton's heart, with many characters borrowing from the biographies of people in his own family—with one, Mark, borrowing from Edgerton himself.

Most of Edgerton's fiction, which includes ten novels and numerous short stories, is set in small-town North Carolina, a place he knows well from his upbringing and later life. Edgerton grew up in Bethesda, N.C., a community not too far from Durham in the North Carolina piedmont. After earning his undergraduate degree from the University of North Carolina at Chapel Hill, he served as a fighter pilot in the U.S. Air Force, then returned to his alma mater for graduate study. It was not until several years after he had received his doctorate and was teaching at Campbell University that Edgerton gave serious thought to writing fiction, inspired in part by his love for Eudora Welty's fiction. Besides at Campbell University, Edgerton has taught at St. Andrew's Presbyterian College, as well as at the University of North Carolina at Wilmington, where he is currently the Thomas S. Kenan III Distinguished Professor and one of the anchors of the Department of Creative Writing. Awards that he has garnered include the Lyndhurst Prize, a Guggenheim Fellowship, the North Carolina Award for Literature, the Thomas Wolfe Prize, and membership in the Fellowship of Southern Writers.

The Floatplane Notebooks explores the rich history and inner workings of the Copeland family, as its various members struggle with both everyday concerns and catastrophes from 1956 to 1971. Told through alternating speakers, the novel follows the family's youngest generation, a wildly diverse group, as they navigate through childhood, adolescence, and young adulthood. There are escapades and challenges, jealousies and heartbreak, rollicking humor and haunting tragedy, and as the novel progresses we are drawn more and more into the characters' efforts to achieve fulfillment and reconciliation, with themselves and with their loved ones. The family patriarch, Albert Copeland, who for years has been lovingly tinkering with a floatplane that he has built from an incomplete kit, perhaps best represents the family's often misguided but endearing eccentricities; and the floatplane itself, pieced together and precariously wobbly, suggests the instability of the family itself, tested time and again by disruptions and threats from within and without.

Haunting the Copeland family's contemporary wranglings are those from its oftentimes dark past, stretching back to pre–Civil War days and told to us by, of all things, an age-old wisteria vine planted next to the family cemetery. You've never heard a wisteria vine speak? Well, you will in *The Floatplane Notebooks;* and you will also discover that at every blue moon the dead arise from the Copeland cemetery to talk about themselves and the family. However you feel about this plunge into other-worldliness, the voices of the vine and the long ago dead fill in the Copeland family history, a history that suggests, as Faulkner famously put it in *Absalom, Absalom!,* "Maybe nothing ever happens once and is finished." That is, maybe the effects of a person's actions don't end with the actions themselves, but ripple forward long into the future, passing from one generation to the next.

The Floatplane Notebooks is a rich and complex novel that reveals so piercingly what we already know about ourselves and our families: that just beneath the calm surfaces roil forces always threatening to erupt. The origins of these forces may stretch into the distant past, but their potency is sustained by the passionate longings and pursuits that make us who we truly are, no matter what composed faces we present to the world.

Robert H. Brinkmeyer, Jr.

INTRODUCTION

In the winter of 1977, during semester break from my new job as an assistant professor of education, I wrote my first short story. I was thirty-three.

Though I had written bad poetry, many student essays, a few sketches, and a Ph.D. thesis, I'd only dreamed vaguely of writing fiction. One of my joys was reading fiction. Never had I been able to write a story with a beginning, middle, and end.

In the kitchen floor of my home was a soft spot. It creaked when you walked on it. The house had been built in 1930 and was beginning to show its age. I decided to crawl under the house to investigate. Beneath the kitchen floor, I found a well—an open well—with a removable cover. The well was situated exactly under the soft spot.

Back up in the kitchen, I visualized someone falling through the soft spot and into the well. In a story, I decided, the person would need to be someone who deserved it. I thought of my cousin, Gary Edgerton, and my friend, Nicky Burton. Both were troublemakers—well, at least mischief makers—though each of a different sort.

I named my troublemaker/mischief maker Meredith. I'd just seen and heard the actor Burgess Meredith read from Faulkner's *The Reivers* on TV. I decided that the troublemaker falling through the floor and into the well would be the main character but not the narrator of the story. The narrator would be Meredith's cousin or brother. The narrator could say that Meredith deserved to fall down the well because he'd thrown litters of kittens down it in the past. Served him right.

I realize in hindsight that my early conceptions of fiction writing—when I'd sort of dreamed of doing it—did not include real places, like the kitchen in my home. I thought everything had to be made up. I was wrong. Visualizing my real kitchen as I began writing the story of Meredith falling down the well helped me visualize the action, helped me make the story seem real.

And I knew that as soon as Meredith fell through the floor, driven by his own weight, members of my real family would be among the crowd rushing in to see what had happened. Leading the pack was my great-uncle Alfred. I'd heard so many stories about Uncle Alfred that he had years before become one of my favorite uncles, even though he died way before I was born. To Meredith, he was Papa.

[Papa says], "You down there?"
"Where you think I'm at?" The echo hangs in the well.

I called the story "Natural Suspension" and started sending it out for publication in March 1978, three months after I'd written it. But I was an education professor, not a fiction writer.

One night in May, after seeing and hearing Eudora Welty read "Why I Live at the P.O." on NPR, I wrote in a journal, "Tomorrow I will start being a fiction writer." I started writing every day, and a dozen or so stories followed. Unfolding before me, as material for fiction, was my life with family and friends, especially my life as a child. I wrote another story or two—drawn from the same characters I'd used in "Natural Suspension." I realized that I might create a novel from the characters I'd created, but before I could get going on it, another novel materialized. *Raney.*

And then I saw a man named Tom Purcell trying to fly a homebuilt airplane off Lake Wheeler in Raleigh, North Carolina. That sight mesmerized me. I was into my Meredith novel, realizing that in the story I could have Albert Copeland (the character based on my uncle Alfred) build an aircraft from a kit and try to fly it. I realized that I could also somehow get my war experiences as a pilot in Southeast Asia into the story—my deep leftover feelings about all that.

But I was interrupted. My mother fell through a rocking chair without a bottom and *Walking Across Egypt,* a second novel, was born. With practically no labor.

Once *Egypt* was out, I was back on the Meredith novel, and when I finished in 1988, I realized that I'd been on it—off and on—for ten years or so.

When I finished a draft (third-person omniscient point of view), I sent it to Shannon Ravenel, my editor at Algonquin Books, and to Louis Rubin, my publisher. Independently, they told me it was awful and not to show it to anybody. I remember Louis writing, "I wouldn't show this to Shannon yet."

I went back to work, knowing I was into—for me—an important story, with main characters Meredith, Papa, and Mark, a character loosely based on my own biography. I tried another draft from Mark's point of view.

So many translated family stories were coming into the novel, but that was a problem, I began to realize. The story was a little bit in-bred. A breakthrough came when a student appeared in a class I was teaching at St. Andrews College in Laurinburg, North Carolina. Her name was Bliss.

I wanted a character named Bliss. I made one up. (I was thinking: she's just out of high school, in love with Meredith's brother Thatcher, enamored of Thatcher's hardscrabble family, and fond of using adverbs.) Her voice brought the book alive for me.

That's when I realized the only way to tell my novel was with individual voices.

Once that decision was made, everything clicked into place. But I faced a structural problem. Individuals who needed to talk were not all alive. I fixed that with a little trick: a wisteria vine that talked. If Fred Chappell and Mr. Marquez and Toni Morrison could play around with time and space and life and death, so could I.

The wisteria vine would introduce a graveyard where people came to life on blue moon nights. The people would talk, tell stories.

I went the library and checked out hundreds of copies of *The Farmer's Almanac*. I found the date of every blue moon between 1850 and 1980.

I was on the way.

Sometimes I'm asked, "Of all your books, which is your favorite?"

I always say, "That's a hard question to answer, but I can say that if I were in a sinking boat with them all and could save only one, the one I'd save is *The Floatplane Notebooks*."

Clyde Edgerton

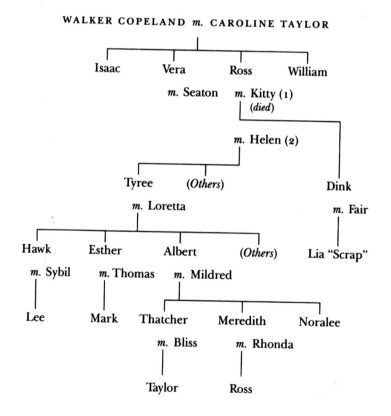

WALKER COPELAND *m.* **CAROLINE TAYLOR**

Isaac   Vera   Ross   William

m. Seaton   *m.* Kitty (1)
(*died*)

m. Helen (2)

Tyree   (*Others*)   Dink

m. Loretta   *m.* Fair

Hawk   Esther   Albert   (*Others*)   Lia "Scrap"

m. Sybil   *m.* Thomas   *m.* Mildred

Lee   Mark   Thatcher   Meredith   Noralee

m. Bliss   *m.* Rhonda

Taylor   Ross

PART ONE

1956–1959

1956

NORALEE

The dogs breathe in my face. They come to me and breathe in my face and turn around and run, then another one comes up and does it. They don't jump on me. If they do, Papa hits them with a piece of water hose.

Mama is pretty. I sleep with my head in her lap while we drive in the car in the night to go see Uncle Hawk. We woke up and started while cars still had their lights on and then in one corner of the sky it got lighter and lighter until the sun came up like a big orange.

My favorite dog is Ben because he is brown and white and that makes him kind. Jack is black and white and has the biggest head of all. Zeb belongs to Mark. Mark pats him on the shoulder all the time. Mark is the only boy who plays the piano. His papa died in a war.

I don't like chicken so I eat apples until we stop and Papa gets mad because I don't eat any chicken. Then I get some vanilla ice cream. Chicken stinks.

I like vanilla ice cream because it's kinder than chocolate. Thatcher is my brother. He washes his car all the time and goes to work to pay for it. Meredith is my other brother.

It takes one whole day to get to Uncle Hawk's. He lives in Florida. Papa gets mad every time I ask him when are we going to get there.

When we stop to let the dogs out, Meredith puts me up on his shoulders and runs with me until Papa hollers. I look down in his curly brown hair while I ride.

Mama is prettier than Aunt Esther. Aunt Esther has gray in her hair. She's Mark's mama.

I like Uncle Hawk. I'll be glad when we get there. Uncle Hawk puts his hand behind his back and holds his arm with his other hand. His hand that is hanging down flaps like a fish while he looks out the window and talks.

I been to Florida every year right after Christmas.

BLISS

My first association with Thatcher's entire family was at their annual gravecleaning last summer. What an event! Cousins, aunts, uncles, and such got together, complete with picnic lunch, and when their work was finished that graveyard was as clean and neat as a whistle.

There is a path—wide enough for a car—which goes down into the woods behind their house, and if you walk or drive on it for a little ways you come to another car path which leads to their family graveyard. There beside the graveyard is a little open grassy area, and beside that is a raging wisteria vine, beyond which is a pond. The graveyard itself is very serene, with shafts of light coming down through tall pines onto the gravestones, which go back into the 1800s. So, one day each summer this wonderful event happens: cousins and such roll up their sleeves, and then cut, mow, trim and rake up a storm.

That was association number one.

Association number two was a trip to Florida, occurring this past Christmas, before our marriage.

I, of course, had no idea that I would ever be going to Florida this early in my life, but Thatcher and I got more and more serious up until November third, when he, at nineteen, asked me to marry him, and I, at eighteen, said I would. My words were, "I will, Thatcher. I will." The words I like to say about Thatcher are these: "Thatcher stands tall." He is slightly over six feet and I think he stands tall not only in stature but in spirit. He has a firmament about him. A steadiness.

They are a wonderful family, full of wonderful family members and names. Isn't Thatcher a fun, but somehow masculine, name? And Meredith, his brother? Doesn't that name have a rolling ring to it? And Noralee, his little sister? Soft and sweet?

The trip to Florida, an annual event for the Copelands, to visit Thatcher's Uncle Hawk and Aunt Sybil, started out on an even-enough keel at four a.m., having to do with lighter traffic in the early morning hours. My parents weren't too happy with the whole idea—they are less enthralled with the Copeland family than I am—but they finally said yes when they found out that Thatcher's aunt, Miss Esther, was going along. Miss Esther is a well-known upholding block of the community.

Speaking of Meredith, Thatcher's thirteen-year-old brother, he is the has-a-sparkle-in-his-eye type, as cute as a button, and always having something up his sleeve. He runs up to me, holds out his hands for me to pop his knuckles, then pretends it hurts terribly. His hair, dark brown, is naturally curly—the only one in the family that way. Along with him on the trip was Mark, a cousin his age, Miss Esther's son. Mark is a very polite young man and spends a good deal of time with Meredith. Mark's father was lost in World War II.

Before we left, Thatcher, Meredith, and Mark told me all about Silver Springs, which is near Locklear, Florida, where Uncle Hawk lives. I, having never been beyond North Carolina, was amazed at their talk of this "Silver Springs"—which was: glass-bottom boats, monkeys in the trees, and catfish playing football with a wad of loafbread underneath said glassbottom boats. And it all did turn out to be true.

Florida definitely has an excitement in the air.

One of the things my parents had a hard time understanding was: anybody taking four bird dogs to Florida.

They were necessary because the men needed to hunt. Two dogs were carried in the trunk of each car, and could get air because the trunks were not completely closed. Old blankets were available for them to lie on. The places we stopped for the dogs to get out—going down and coming back—were little dirt side roads that seemed to be made for the occasion.

Miss Esther drove her car and Mr. Copeland, his.

I loved being on the road, traveling before light, with the one I love.

We arrived in the fairly late afternoon.

Yes, there we were in Florida—a very warm state with a sense of exhilaration which hangs in the air like the very fog.

Uncle Hawk walked out of the front of his store to greet us. He is the oldest and the largest, and Miss Esther, his sister, is, I think, a little older than Mr. Copeland, who is the youngest—Thatcher's daddy, Mr. Albert Copeland. They all look alike too. Uncle Hawk immediately hit Meredith on the shoulder and then grabbed him around the head and spoke loudly, "Boy, you done gone up like a okra stalk." Then he grabbed Thatcher and Mark around their heads and pulled them to his chest with them laughing and enjoying it and then hugged Miss Esther and Mildred and shook hands with Mr. Copeland, pulling on Mr. Copeland's hand and grabbing him by the shoulder and laughing. Then he reached out his hand to me and was exceedingly nice, saying nice things about me, Mildred having written that I'd be coming along on the trip. Then he picked up little Noralee and carried her as we all went inside.

The store is quite an establishment—it's a cafe-grocery-hardware store combination with gas pumps and a large fruit stand out front. Their home is next to the store, across a little side road, surrounded by a rock wall, and with palms and Spanish moss hanging from big oak trees. Very pleasant.

Inside the store we were greeted by my aunt-to-be Sybil. She was carrying a tiny, short-haired dog named Dixie B., which Mr. Copeland had talked about on the way down—saying he hoped she had died.

"Come on in," said Aunt Sybil. She hugged everybody with one arm. She wore frilly lace around her neck and had a pleasant round face. "I'm going to hug you too," she said to me. And did. "Anyone like something to eat?"

"Oh, no," said Miss Esther. "We still got chicken in the car."

Thatcher's mother, a beautiful, thick-brown haired woman who keeps up her fingernails—and who asked me to call her Mildred—said, "What you got today?"

"The usual," said Aunt Sybil. "Tuna, chicken, ham, hamburger, hot dogs."

"I could use a hot dog—without onions," said Mildred.

"What's tuna?" said Meredith. Bless his heart.

"You know what tuna is."

"No, I don't."

"Fish. It's a kind of fish. Comes in a can."

"Ain't you going to school up there, boy?" said Uncle Hawk.

"No sir—I mean yes sir, but we don't study tuna."

Meredith is a regular spark plug.

Sleeping arrangements were available for all. Miss Esther and I settled into the bedroom of Uncle Hawk and Aunt Sybil's daughter, Lee, who lives and works in Kentucky, and had left to go back on the morning of the day we arrived —the day after Christmas. Lee's a social worker and Christmas is one of her busiest times, Aunt Sybil said. I was to sleep on a rollaway bed, Miss Esther on the single bed, Mildred and little Noralee in the living room on a foldout couch.

Mr. Copeland, Thatcher, Meredith, and Mark were to sleep in the guest room built onto the garage, out behind the house. From there they would get up early and go to the fields to hunt. I, of course, did not visit Thatcher in those quarters, nor did I wish to.

The first night, we watched television for a while in the living room, then Aunt Sybil said maybe we ought to turn off the television and talk a little bit, catch up, which Miss Esther agreed with.

One of the first things Uncle Hawk wanted to talk about was the floatplane kit which Mr. Copeland bought from Mr.

Hoover, who is going to teach Mr. Copeland to fly—in exchange for hickory shavings that Mr. Copeland gets from the sawmill he runs. The Anderson Sawmill. Mr. Hoover has a restaurant and cooks barbecue with the hickory shavings.

"How big is the thing, Albert?" asked Uncle Hawk.

"Twenty feet—the fuselage—the middle part is called the fuselage, and the wing span is thirty-four feet. She can sit one or two. I'm using the two option. It's called a floatplane. Fly it off the water."

"Mr. Hoover said all the pages to the plans weren't there," said Mildred.

"It's mostly aluminum tubing," said Mr. Copeland. "I'll fly it off the lake."

"What kind of engines?" asked Uncle Hawk.

"All the plans aren't there?" said Aunt Sybil.

"I'll find them. I just got me a notebook to keep up with all I'm doing right now, what I do to it, and the test runs. That's required by law—the FAA. It's an experimental aircraft."

"He don't write it accurate about what happened though," said Thatcher.

"I do too."

"Not on that first test run."

"Well I sure did."

Thatcher said one thing happened at the lake, but when Mr. Copeland wrote it down it sounded quite different.

NORALEE

I was sitting under the tree when they came out of the house and went into the shop, so I followed them. They got the floatplane down off the table to load it on the boat trailer. The wings were folded back against the sides. It had two propellers in front. Papa had screwed two lawn chairs in it where you sit.

"Can I go?" I said.

"You need to stay here with your mama," said Papa.

Mama came out the back door. "How do you know it'll float?" she said.

"It'll float."

"Joe Ray Hoover said—"

"It'll float. I ain't worried about it floating."

"If it sinks," said Thatcher, "that's a hundred and thirty dollars of chain-saw engines on the bottom of Lake Blanca."

Thatcher and Meredith painted it red.

"That's the last thing I'm worried about," says Papa.

"Why can't I go?" I said.

"You ain't old enough," said Meredith.

"I am too. I'm five."

"You'll be in the way."

I wanted to see what all would happen. "Please, Papa. I won't be in the way."

"Let her go," said Mama. "You need somebody there to run for help."

They let me go. They said they were going to zip it around on the lake. They let me ride in the back of the truck. They all rode in the front. The dogs rode in back with me.

We had a long ride to Lake Blanca. Papa drove slow. It was a sunny day and we were just riding along pulling it behind us down the road with people passing us.

When we got it to the lake, a lot of people came around and watched them get it down in the water. Meredith and Thatcher had on their bathing suits and were down in the water and Papa was standing on the plank thing that goes out in the water. Meredith just got to be a teenager.

More and more people came up and Meredith and Thatcher got out of the water.

"Who's going with me first?" said Papa. He was standing on the wood thing and he was holding the wing.

Meredith said he would.

Because the wing was in the way they couldn't get it close enough to the wood thing you stand on to get in it. Then they got it turned the right way and got in. Papa told Thatcher to hold the tail while he started it up. It was sunk down low with him and Meredith both in there. Papa sent Thatcher to the truck to get the lawnmower rope to start it with. The little rope with the little wood handle and a knot in the end. A man who walked out there was holding the floatplane while Thatcher went and got the rope. I was staying in the back of the truck like Papa told me.

Thatcher and the man held on to the tail while Papa tried to start a engine but it wouldn't start. Then he wrapped the rope around the little thing on the other engine and jerked it and it started. It was the one in front of Meredith. It was running real fast and made a lot of noise and the plane was pulling on Thatcher and the man. The dogs were standing there barking. Papa told them to turn loose. When they turned loose the plane started out in this big circle. The engine was real loud. Papa was pointing down under the front inside, and hollering at Meredith. The plane was turning in a big circle back around toward the wood thing where the man was. The dogs were still barking and standing on the wood thing. The man started running back onto the land. Papa bended down and I couldn't see him no more. The plane was going in a big circle but it was headed toward the wood thing. Meredith stood up. He bended over like he was talking to Papa. He jumped out.

The airplane kept in the circle and missed the thing you stand on. It kept going in a big circle and was headed back around right at Meredith so he started swimming fast and looking back over his shoulder. It looked like it was going to miss him but it—Papa was down inside working on it—it straightened out all of a sudden and came right at Meredith and he just waited for it and when it got to him he dived under water. Then Papa stood up and when he sat down it was headed straight for the land. When it hit the land it sort of flipped Papa up to the front and then back. He put safety belts in it when we got home. The dogs ran up around him barking. The motor shut off and they quit barking. Fox and Trader.

Thatcher told Mama when we got home that if Papa had been going any faster he would have cut his head off in the propeller when he hit the land. But he wouldn't have, because he was on the side where the engine didn't start.

THATCHER

This floatplane thing Papa's working on. I swear. The frame is a bunch of aluminum pipes that fit together, and it's on pontoons so it'll fly off a lake.

Papa says by the time he's finished building it he'll have all his flying lessons from Mr. Hoover, who has an instructor's license and instructs part-time at the airport. Then he'll fly it off Lake Blanca.

My ass. He's taken it to the lake once to try it out on the water and it just turned in these two big circles and ended up *grounding* itself. Meredith jumped out.

So when we get home that afternoon Papa writes in his notebook. It says "Record" on the front. He had the date, the temperature, the wind direction, the altitude of the lake, which he said was sea level—hell, I got more sense than that —and then this:

NARRATIVE ACCOUNT: THE EXPERIMENTAL AIRCRAFT WAS TOWED TO LAKE BLANCA BEHIND OWNERS JEEP TRUCK.

ALONG FOR THE OCCASION WAS THE OWNER, SONS MERE-
DITH COPELAND AND THATCHER COPELAND. DAUGHTER
NORALEE COPELAND AND TWO ANIMALS, FOX AND TRADER
(DOG NAMES). THE AIRCRAFT FLOATED LEVEL IN THE WATER
AND WAS RUN SUCCESSFUL OUT ON THE WATER AND BACK
IN. THIS WAS THE FIRST TEST RUN. PASSENGERS WERE THE
OWNER AND SON MEREDITH. ALL PARTS WORKED.

Then it's got Meredith's and Mark's and Noralee's weights
and heights. I'd be in there but I'm grown.

"Papa," I said, "you wrote up in that notebook that it was a
successful test run. Couldn't much more have gone wrong
except if it blowed up."

"What are you talking about?" he says.

"You wrote down that it was successful."

"It was."

"But it ran around in circles and one of the engines
wouldn't start!"

"The rudder was caught."

"I know. But you didn't write that down, and about the
engine not starting."

"No need to. I got it straightened out. That's why I didn't
write it down. I got it straightened out."

"But you're supposed to write down what happened."

"What happened was I fixed the rudder, and now the
engine starts. I'll write that in later. There's no need to write
about all that for the test run. Just the simple facts."

"Papa, that's . . . why you got them weights and heights and
birthdays in there?"

"So they won't get lost."

"What will the FAA say if you got all—"

"It's a record. That's all it is. I'm keeping it. It's my record. You want a record of something, *you* write it up. But don't you go complaining about *my* record or how I keep it, or I'll hide it. You ain't no government official."

I asked him later about the lake being at sea level and he said all water has to be at sea level. You can't tell him nothing.

BLISS

Mr. Copeland was explaining about a company in Michigan that modified chain-saw engines for use on airplanes when Uncle Hawk stood and said, "I got to feed the dogs. Who wants to come?"

I can't get over the importance of dogs to this family.

Mr. Copeland, Meredith, and Mark went along and Thatcher reluctantly followed, wanting to be with me, I firmly believe, yet not wanting, I suppose, to be the only man left inside among several women.

They went out the back door. I momentarily harbored the thought of going with Thatcher out into the night to feed the dogs, but relinquished it.

"Well, how about you, Bliss?" says Aunt Sybil, turning to me. "Where did you get a lovely name like that?"

"It was my grandmother's name. She died before I was born."

"I think it's wonderful to keep names in the family. We

named Lee after my sister, who had died a year to the day before Lee was born. Poor thing had a stroke and there is not the slightest history of stroke in the family. When's the wedding?"

"Next spring. May fifth. The day after the gravecleaning. Mr. Copeland suggested that—so you and Uncle Hawk would be up there too."

"Well, that's just wonderful. Thatcher is such a nice young man. And I've been watching him grow up since he weren't bigger than nothing."

In the back door comes all the men with the addition of a Dan Braddock, whom I had heard some talk about, but whom I had yet to meet. I knew he was Uncle Hawk's partner at the store, but wasn't around too much because of his other businesses.

They came in and Uncle Hawk pulled in another chair from the dining room. Dan Braddock hugged a few necks, took a seat, and went into talking about his business. His appearance was singular. Most noticeable was his belt being extraordinarily high, with the main portion of his stomach below his belt buckle. He had a big, fat, red face, a Stetson hat, which he did not remove, but instead pushed back on his head. He had this noticeable manner of looking around at everybody without ever lighting down on one person. He went into talking about "the old days" and started using curse words and told about cheating the town of Lubbock, Texas, out of four thousand dollars on a land deal and about how he wanted to get into the real estate business full time.

Miss Esther suddenly stands up and says she wants to go on back to get ready for bed. I also stood, knowing the language was getting too rough for my ears. Then Miss Esther told Mark he ought to go out and get ready for bed. Mark looked at Meredith, Meredith looked at his mother, Mildred, and said, "I want to stay."

"Am I talking too strong for the kids?" asked Mr. Braddock. I myself certainly thought so.

"Yes, I suppose. A little, I think," said Miss Esther.

"It's too bad Thomas didn't live through the war," Mr. Braddock said to Miss Esther. "You'd a had to get used to it."

"Thomas never cheated nobody, Dan, and if he did he didn't laugh about it."

"Well," said Mr. Braddock, "I understand he might have cheated somebody."

Miss Esther didn't say anything. She stood there staring at him for about five or ten seconds and then walked on into the bedroom.

As I departed, I noticed that Mr. Braddock's eyes were darting around the room looking at everybody, and as I walked into the bedroom, Miss Esther called out to Mark to go on out and get ready to go to bed. "Now," she said.

I then prepared for bed, hoping I would sleep well in strange circumstances.

I felt it would be appropriate to say something because Miss Esther seemed a little . . . I suppose *flustered* is the best word. So I said, "Your family is very interesting."

"They are. They are," she replied. "Hawk's always been as good as he could be. Giving people things. Taking on Dan like he did, as a business partner, and then Dan turning out like he did." As she turned back her sheet I noticed her hand was shaking.

I turned back the sheet on my rollaway bed. "Your husband was named Thomas?"

"Yes. Thomas Carl . . . Thomas Carl Oakley."

Next morning was Silver Springs—and it was all I had dreamed and more.

The glass-bottom boats were exquisite. What a sight looking down into those underwater caverns! What exquisite underwater scenery! And just as was promised, the guide, upon encountering a school of catfish, threw a ball of white bread over the side, and as we watched through that glass boat-bottom, the catfish chased the bread all over the place, one and then the other running with it and all of this in this exquisite underwater world where the water was so very clear—as if it were all happening in the very sky. It was as if the very sky were below you, open and naked.

And to top it all off, there was a man at Silver Springs named Ross Allen who *milked* rattlesnakes, putting the rim of a glass into a rattlesnake's mouth and causing venom to squirt into the glass, a few drops, enough to kill a human being.

What a good, good time!

After the men came in from hunting on each of the next three afternoons, Thatcher and I would have a little time to talk alone at a table in the cafe section. He'd tell me all about the hunt. He was very excited on all three days, and would have that safari look which I adore in a man, especially Thatcher who stands so tall and looks so handsome in anything he wears, and Meredith of course would be trying to

23

tell me all these things that happened on the hunt, and Thatcher, bless his heart, would want to be alone with me at the table—as I did want to be alone with him, while at the same time I found Meredith a joy. So finally Meredith and Mark would go out under the shed in the back of the store where Uncle Hawk and Mr. Copeland were cleaning birds.

The spectacle of a bird cleaning is something to behold: feathers and birds' insides all over the place, with the cats, Ford and Plymouth, sitting nearby—watching and waiting intently—waiting for the spoils of battle to come flinging their way.

Thatcher explained how, in the early morning before the hunt, Uncle Hawk comes to the foot of their bed before light and holds their feet until they wake up. Then he comes on over to the store while they get dressed. Then they walk across the road in the dark and in through the back door of the store where Uncle Hawk is cooking breakfast, pretending he's Old Ross, his granddaddy, and singing while he cooks breakfast like Old Ross used to. Old Ross was Thatcher's great-granddaddy and died back before Thatcher was born. Thatcher's granddaddy, Tyree, used to do the same thing at breakfast—sing like his daddy. Now Uncle Hawk pretends he's Old Ross and he sings.

Thatcher also told me on the second day that they'd killed a rattlesnake. Horrors!

We said our warm goodbyes and left without incident on the fifth morning at about six a.m. We drove through some pretty country in Florida, with the trees far apart. I like it with space between the trees. And on up through Georgia and South Carolina.

At some point when we stopped to let the dogs out, and Thatcher and I were relatively alone, I asked him what Dan Braddock meant when he made the comment about Mark's father cheating. Thatcher said nobody ever talked about it but it had to do with "another woman" overseas during the war. That's all he knew. I wondered about it, but also recalled the wisdom of that old saying, "Let bygones be bygones."

We finally arrived home without event. My mother said she was relieved the trip was over. She said it with an attitude which led me to believe she didn't grasp the force with which Thatcher and I were in love.

MARK

When we were driving back from Florida, Aunt Mildred told Bliss about finding the drowned kitten that time. That was back when me and Meredith were little. She pulled up the kitten out of the well in the water bucket. Meredith done it—drowned a whole litter. Me and him were playing marbles when she pulled it up. She screams, "Oh, my God," looks down into the well and says, "Are they all down there?" She unhooks the bucket from the well rope—it's got water and the kitten in it—and walks to the tool shed. Meredith and me follow her. She gets a shovel, goes behind the tool shed, sets the water bucket on the ground, digs a hole, and pours the water and the kitten into the hole. The kitten floats, then the water seeps down in the ground, leaving him in the hole, sopping wet, with white skin where his fur is parted. Meredith and me stand there watching. Aunt Mildred covers him up and steps on top of the dirt, which sinks down with her footprints in it over and over. "Where's Thatcher?"

she says. "He was supposed to drown those kittens in the pond."

Then when Uncle Albert comes home, and Thatcher says he didn't do it, that he gave them to Meredith to do it, Uncle Albert finds us.

"Did you drop them kittens down that well, Meredith?"

"No sir."

"Well, who did?"

"Mark."

"I did not! That's a story! *You* did! You held them by the neck and dropped them!"

"Sit down on that root," says Uncle Albert. "Both of you. Thatcher, Noralee, come sit on this root right this minute."

We all sit. Uncle Albert walks back and forth. He is short and always wears loose overalls. He talks, walking back and forth. Finally he says, "Mark, you go home and tell your mama I'm going to whip you and Meredith and Thatcher. I'll be waiting right here."

When I get home I can't get my breath to talk because I'm crying so hard. Mother's looking in the refrigerator when I walk in, and then I am holding onto her, crying. I can look through the window and see that they are standing there waiting for me.

Mother walks with me outside to the tree. "What happened?" she says.

"These boys drowned some cats in the wrong place—in the damn well—and I aim to whip mine and I'll whip yourn if you're a mind."

"I ain't a mind," says Mother. "I'll tend to Mark."

We walk back home. Mother walks with her hand on my

head. Meredith hollers that he is going to beat me up. Uncle Albert tells him to be quiet.

I stand at the window and see Uncle Albert talk to them some more and then send them after switches. Then I see him whip them with their pants down, bending over.

Mother sees me looking and tells me to get away from the window. Then she tells me it's wrong to drop kittens down the well, but that she knows I didn't do it, and for me not to ever tell a story.

The other worse time when Meredith lied was when he started the welldigger and got me to lie too. It was all his fault. I just thought we were going to camp out, that's all.

Mother was out on the back porch potting a plant. There was a big, flat black cloud, churning up into itself, but below it you could see the sun setting like a full moon.

"Mother, can I still camp out?" I say. "Uncle Albert says the rain's all blowed around."

"We'll have to see, son. Oh, look! Mark, look at that sunset. Oh, I don't think I've ever seen one so beautiful. And look what it does to the crepe myrtle."

"Can I, Mother?"

"Look! Come here. Look at that. Isn't that beautiful?"

"Yes ma'am. Can I?"

"Is it going to be just you and Meredith?"

"Yes ma'am."

"In the backyard?"

"Yes ma'am."

"Well, if you'll practice your music, and that cloud goes away. But you can't go off. And if you-all want breakfast in the morning, you come in and eat. I'll fix you some break-fast. Meredith ain't old enough to cook yet. He's liable to burn hisself."

So I practice my piano music. I'm playing these songs I don't like very much. Minuets and stuff. Meredith thinks it's sissy. I mash on the soft pedal so he won't hear it from out-side. I think about what if I could play boogie-woogie songs like Miss Paulson does after church on Wednesday nights sometimes. I see people standing around me when I finish playing some boogie-woogie, smiling at me, telling me how wonderful it was, what a beautiful way I played it, and there is a girl there, waiting for me, who falls in love with me, and then if I die she'll kneel down over me and be dressed in a white dress.

Meredith is putting up the tent on the grass beside the garden over in his backyard.

"Was that you playing?" he says.

"Yeah. I hadn't practiced today."

Later, we are lying in the tents on our stomachs, looking at the fire, which is almost out.

We talk about what we are going to do when we grow up. Meredith says he's going to be a truck driver and a pilot. I say I'm going to be a doctor and a pilot.

Meredith asks me about my daddy, and says that his mother told his aunt Joanne from Ohio that my daddy had a French girlfriend when he was in the Army. Meredith says it's okay because you can do whatever you want to when you're in the Army.

I tell him it's not true about my daddy, and that you have to follow the rules when you're in the Army.

29

Then Meredith says we ought to go over and sit in the welldigger in his yard—and pretend it's an Army tank. They're digging a new well. I say okay but I feel worried.

We go through the darkness, across Meredith's yard to the welldigger. When we get there he shines his flashlight on it. "Let's get up in front," he says.

We climb up into the truck cab. Meredith sits behind the steering wheel. "Let's turn on the well-digging part," he says. He takes the key from a wire hanging on the mirror. We get out and walk in the dark around to the back of the truck. Meredith shines the flashlight on the motor until he finds the key slot. He sticks the key in the slot. It is almost as high as he can reach. He holds the flashlight with his other hand. "They turn the key, then click that switch over there and it starts." He turns the key. "Click it."

"You click it."

"Well, hold the flashlight then." Meredith hands me the flashlight and clicks the switch. The machine cranks with this rattling, cranking, popping noise. I turn out the flashlight and start running, stop, then start again—toward the tent. I have to run past Meredith's house to get back to the tent. Meredith hollers at me: "Bring the flashlight back!" But I keep running. Lights come on at Uncle Albert's. The front door opens. I click off the flashlight, duck into a corn row and lay on my stomach and watch. I feel the sand under my belt buckle against my skin, and wet grass blades against my arm. I'm afraid to move.

Uncle Albert comes out onto the porch and stands under the light bulb. He is in his pajamas, and barefooted. His legs are bowed and his fists balled. "Meredith!"

Meredith don't answer. The welldigger sounds like hundreds of pots and pans. Uncle Albert starts down the steps, then turns and goes back in the house. Meredith comes running by me. I call him. He stops, comes back, and ducks into the corn row with me.

"Come on," he says. "We got to get out of here."

Uncle Albert, now dressed, comes out onto the porch and yells: "Meredith!"

Meredith drops down beside me.

Aunt Mildred and Thatcher come onto the porch. They start toward the welldigger.

We crawl along the corn row, headed for the far end of the garden.

Meredith says, "Let's go follow them." I stop, then I follow him. We hide behind a line of bushes, close to the welldigger.

Uncle Albert shines the light on the motor in back, finds the switch and turns it off. The welldigger shakes to a stop.

They start back toward the house; we go running through the garden to the tent. When we get to the tent a light comes on in my house. We duck into the tent and sit on the blankets.

"Where did you go?" asked Meredith.

"I was getting out of there."

"I couldn't see how to turn it off. You chicken."

"I am not. Why'd you start it up?"

"To see if it would."

"He's going to know you did it."

"No, he won't. Get under here and play like you're asleep."

We get under the blankets.

Uncle Albert, Aunt Mildred, and Thatcher walk up to the tent.

31

"Meredith?" says Uncle Albert. "Come out here."

Meredith throws back his blanket. I don't move. He crawls out.

"Meredith, how come this fresh mud is tracked across here and how come you got mud all over your boots? How come you wearing your boots?"

"We tried to catch a nigger trying to start up the welldigger and then we came back here. That's all."

"That's a joke," says Thatcher. "You done it sure as day. You lie."

I can kind of see a nigger in my mind. "Yeah," I say, crawling out.

"Let's go to bed," said Mildred, "and talk about it tomorrow. It won't nothing but them starting up the welldigger, and now it's turned off. Don't crank it up no more, Meredith. And you boys quit fibbin'—your nose'll fall off."

Mother walks up. "What's going on?"

"Somebody started up the welldigger," says Thatcher.

"I heard it," said Mother. "Have you been away from that tent, Mark?"

"Yes ma'am, we had to . . . to try to see who started the welldigger over there."

"I told you not to leave that tent."

"We had to go try to find out who it was," says Meredith, "and it was a nigger. A big nigger. So we came back. It was. Whether you believe it or not. It was a nigger. Big."

"I'm going to bed," says Mildred, starting to the house. "Good night."

Mother makes us go inside and sleep in my room. Meredith sleeps on a mattress on the floor. We talk some before we go to sleep and I look through the window screen at the mimosa tree and the stars in the black sky, and wish we were outside.

Those were two times Meredith lied. I don't tell lies. Except I did that time about the welldigger, but it was because of Meredith, and I got to thinking about it. I thought about the nigger until I could see him in the darkness by the welldigger, moving slowly, white eyes in the dark, moving in the darkness around to the far side of the welldigger. The nigger had been there. Jesus would still love me if the nigger had been there and he probably had been. He could have been there, but in case he hadn't been there at all, I prayed: "Jesus, I'm sorry—if the nigger won't there. I think he might have been there, though. Dear Jesus, I'm sorry—if the nigger won't there."

33

1957

BLISS

I'm so glad our wedding could be the day after the grave-cleaning so Uncle Hawk and Aunt Sybil could be here for both, and not have to make two trips.

My parents thought the idea was odd, while I supported it fully because it made perfect sense to me. I was therefore left somewhat secluded in my own family since they didn't agree with the general procedure.

"The wedding should be the whole event," said my mother, sitting at our dining room table, drinking coffee and smoking one of her Pall Malls. "I've never heard of such a thing."

"Mother, they're a wonderful family. And this is a wonderful tradition."

"I thought they stopped doing that in the last century."

"What's the matter?" said my father, walking up to stand in the doorway. He's a handsome man who pouts sometimes.

Mother replied, looking at him over her shoulder, elbow

on table, cigarette in hand: "They want to have the wedding
and a gravecleaning at the same time."

"Who? A what?"

"The Copelands."

"No, they don't," I said. "Not at the same time. They
want the gravecleaning one day and the wedding the next,
so Uncle Hawk and Aunt Sybil can make just one trip instead
of two."

"Uncle 'Hawk'?" said Father.

"I told you about him."

"Sounds like an Indian chief."

"So we're having to move the wedding up," stated Mother
to Father.

"A month," I said. "That's not much."

"That's a lot," said Mother. "You don't know what's involved
in planning a wedding."

"Why couldn't they move the damn gravecleaning?" said
Father.

"It's a tradition," I said. "They always do it the first Saturday in May."

"Oh, great." My father turned and walked away. "I didn't
know they had traditions," he said in the hallway.

I am overcome with the black valley between my family
and the family of my husband-to-be. There seems to be no
bridge in sight. Oh, but for a bridge. We even lack an ade-
quate bridge inside my family. My sister Claire is practically
not in our family. She works in Hoover, Alabama, and we
never hear from her.

But if there isn't a bridge? "Happy go lucky," I always say.
Although I love my mother and father dearly, I must not be

deflected, when such an exciting new, additional family is in my grasp.

So the whole graveyard-wedding weekend was one of merriment and good cheer. My mother and father stayed, thankfully, in the background somewhat.

It all started with the arrival on Friday (the gravecleaning was on Saturday; the wedding, Sunday) of Uncle Hawk, Aunt Sybil, and—I don't know why—Dan Braddock, who right away told three or four ugly jokes about honeymoons. The three of them drove the distance in Uncle Hawk's used black Cadillac.

Uncle Hawk had two flat tires on the way up from Florida, and at supper he went into a separate story with all the details about changing each one. Then he started telling stories about when they were growing up. They all lived right here at the graveyard until sometime in the thirties when the old road got closed off and a new road came through at a different place.

Saturday, May fourth, gravecleaning day, broke hot. Thatcher stood tall. He was dressed in blue jeans and a white T-shirt. I had fixed lemonade and brownies as my portion. Miss Esther had told me not to worry, but I insisted. I wanted to be immersed in the whole tradition of the gravecleaning and all that went with it, which included, of course, the women preparing the food while the men handled problems such as, on this particular gravecleaning: a large dead tree which had fallen across the graveyard and had to be axed into sections and then hauled away in Mr. Copeland's truck.

39

By ten o'clock a large contingent of family had arrived at Thatcher's house—about twenty people, and four or five dogs. Mark and Meredith each brought a mixed-breed dog, Fox and Trader, who, in turn, brought several friends along. Everybody had people their age to match up with, plus there were several old people. Mildred took me around and introduced me to everybody. I finally got to meet Aunt Scrap, one of the older cousins I'd heard so much about. She has a wrinkled face, is somewhat stooped and wore a red bandanna around her head. Her eyes were little slits like a Japanese, almost.

All the rakes, hoes, and other implements, and picnic lunches were placed in the back of Mr. Copeland's jeep truck; he drove ahead to the graveyard while all others walked along the path through the woods. Thatcher and I held hands and I soaked up the beauty of the woods, especially the dogwood trees.

And as we walk along the final path I see a horrific splendor of purple wisteria blooms off to the left of the graveyard—a far larger gathering of such blooms than I have ever witnessed. Thatcher had shown me the graveyard and we'd walked down there several times. In fact, I'd walked down there and cried the time Thatcher took Veronica Harden out to lunch, but I had not really noticed the wisteria, since it hadn't been in bloom those times. The vines cover an area about the size of four or five houses, running out and around the limbs of tall stately pine trees and also uniformly winding very tightly up their trunks, eventually to kill them, I fear; thus a mixture of splendor and dread such as you would never expect to find in the very woods down behind Thatcher's house.

Mr. Copeland was already there, chopping with an ax on the large pine tree—fallen partly across the graveyard—so it could be taken to the pickup, a piece at a time.

Everyone started in to work, except Noralee and several of the smaller children, who walked down to the edge of the pond, which is beyond the wisteria. Mr. Copeland will not let them swim in the pond until after June first.

Miss Esther started in helping Mr. Copeland tote pieces of the log away. She works like a man. I got a hedge clipper and joined in, clipping a hedge planted near the center of the graveyard.

Aunt Scrap talked most of the time. We hadn't been working long when she came over to me. She was holding a rake—a yard rake, the kind with the short, straight, hard prongs. She leaned on the handle. Fresh tiny rivers of snuff juice were in the corners of her mouth. "Well, well," she said. "You're Bliss."

"Yes ma'am."

"You know what kind of bush that is?"

"No ma'am."

"It's a Sweet Betsy bush, come from T. C. Sutton's place about the time they tore it down. When they closed off that road used to run through here, things kind of died out. People moved out; houses got torn down. Anyway, Sweet Betsy —Mrs. Sutton had them all over her front yard. Don't trim quite so close there."

"Okay."

"That Thatcher's a fine boy."

"Thank you."

"He's my, let's see, I guess second cousin. His granddaddy

41

and my daddy were half brothers. You know"—she looked down, then up at me—"on this marriage stuff, they told me if I swallowed a raw quail heart I'd marry the first beau to come along and talk to me, and I knew the time of day Horace Jacobs walked along the road, that road that was right out there." She pointed. "So I saved one and swallowed it—just before I knowed it was time for him to come along. I lived about half a mile down that way. And sure enough there he come and I made myself noticeable right out in the front yard. We got married too." She laughed. She was leaning forward, looking at me, and her eyebrows were raised. Then she turned and spat a stream onto the ground where she'd already raked. She looked out over the graveyard. "Lord amercy. There's a bunch of good people in the ground here. And there ought not to be 'ary another one added."

"There's some more room back there, isn't there?" I asked.

She looked up at me. "Sure is, but it's been a good while—thirty years or more—and people just sort of started getting buried at church graveyards, and so that makes this like a little museum. You wouldn't put a new piece of furniture in a museum, would you?"

"I don't guess so."

"You hear about how this graveyard got started?"

"No ma'am."

"Well, it was when my great-granddaddy and grandmother, Walker and Caroline, lived here, and my granddaddy was a little boy, Ross. He was a pistol, that Ross. I remember him. He had a great big mustache when he died, 1918, buried right over there. He was something. He had real light blue eyes which got lighter and lighter and when he died they were almost white. His nose was sort of up-tilted, which is why he grew that mustache, and when he got old his galluses held up pants so big at the waist he looked like he was standing in a barrel. He was the one lived his whole life in that house that was right there. He remembered when the graveyard got started, too. I heard him talk about it. What happened was a field hand died. This was a cotton field and the field hand dropped dead, and they buried him on the spot. Didn't have no family. Fellow by the name of Pittman. He's buried right there. Unmarked. Then somebody else died, somebody's baby I think. Most of the ones unmarked, them over there, are infant graves. And there's the little rock that says 'Born Ded' on it. Ross carved that on there. Come here, and I'll show you."

We walked over to a small stone, about the size of a football, but flatter, and sure enough, there it was, chipped into it: "Born Ded."

"Then of course that tombstone there is Tyree and Loretta and over there is Ross and Helen and his other wife and then there is Walker and Caroline, the ones that buried the field hand. My mama and papa are buried back there in that back row: Dink and Fair. And then all these others." She shook pine straw off the rake. "Oh yes, and Vera. She collected a Confederate pension—her husband got killed in the Civil War. Can't remember his name. She lived alone, and chickens roosted on her bed. She was a laudanum addick. Would drink that stuff and dance up a storm. She wore a bunch of petticoats and had great big pockets in her aprons. She'd walk nine miles to get that laudanum when she was, Lord, over seventy years old, I guess. My, my. Course you're not old enough to be interested in all this yet."

"Oh, yes ma'am, I—"

"Then too, it ain't your blood kin."

"Oh, yes ma'am, I am interested," I said.

I thus found myself looking into the eyes of one of the very backbones and spirits of this marvelous family, which continues even unto today—witness Mr. and Mrs. Copeland, Meredith, Noralee, and now Thatcher and me—unabated into the future.

I think about my mother and father's parents and grandparents, buried in large conventional cemeteries—so unromantically—without an entire enclave, an entire force as it were, buried all around them. It seems to me that the tradition of being buried here should be renewed. It's the most peaceful place imaginable: the pond, the wisteria, the majestic pine trees.

"When the house stood over there," said Aunt Scrap, "right over there, my great-grandma, Caroline, planted that wisteria plant by the back steps. She had seven or eight names—I used to could say them. Course I won't born when she planted it, but I do remember when it grew back there, trimmed —beside the back steps, up a trellis. Then it come up by the pond and they'd let it go, then trim it back, then let it go, and now look at that. You let one of them wisterias get loose and it's gone every which way. They'll never get that one back under control. They're the meanest plants you ever seen." She called to Meredith, "Get that dog off that grave. He looks like he's about to take a notion to dig."

"Ain't my dog."

"I don't care whose dog it is. Get him off there."

THE VINE

I was planted as a seedling by the back steps soon after first light on the day the field hand died planted by a woman named Cora Rosa Hunter Novella Caroline Hildred Martha Bird Taylor Copeland. Her husband Walker called her Puss. Others called her Caroline.

She dug a hole by the back steps with the piece of a grub hoe she used for her flowers. It was very early in the morning and cool. Beyond the pasture and the pond a wisp of low fog flung along just dipping into the tops of trees.

Walker called from inside. Puss where you?

Out here planting a wisteria.

Walker stepped onto the back porch stopped pulled his suspender straps over his shoulders.

Caroline pressed loose dirt with her foot. It'll have a chance to get a good start before it gets too hot. I want to get something started back here. And I want you or Isaac one to build a trellis.

45

Caroline walked over into the kitchen and started a fire to cook breakfast. The children Isaac Vera and Ross the smallest came out of the house and went briefly to their spots in the woods. When they came back Vera washed her hands with water from a pan on the porch and then pulled up a cloth-covered pail of milk from the well.

Ross looked around then picked up a rock and threw it at a chicken as a man came out of the smokehouse. Thomas Pittman the field hand.

Don't do that Thomas Pittman said.

Ross frowned and went into the kitchen.

Thomas Pittman took breakfast in the yard sitting with his back against a tree.

They finished eating and the children and Walker fed the animals then they all went to the field.

Before the sun was straight above Walker rolled Thomas Pittman back into the yard in a wheelbarrow one foot dragging.

Ross was with Walker. He stood watching as Walker with difficulty got Thomas Pittman up onto the back porch and laid him down went inside got a long coat covered the body down to just below the knees then said to Ross Now you stay here and watch him. Don't let the dogs get at him. And shell that there pan of peas while you're at it.

Yessir.

Walker stared at the covered corpse scratched himself then started back to the field.

Ross sat on the back steps and looked for a while at the shape of Thomas Pittman under the coat. Then he stood and walked with long bouncing strides over into the kitchen.

Two bird dog puppies ran from around the corner of the house. One stopped squatted peed then scrambled up the steps toward the corpse. The other one followed. The first approached the head of the corpse bit and held the coat at Thomas Pittman's head growled shook it back and forth and moved backward uncovering the head. The other puppy started for Thomas Pittman's pale face stopped wagged his tail and suddenly reared onto his hind legs then went for the ear licked it bounded back bounded forward again and licked the neck below the ear then started barking.

Ross came running. Git away from there. Git. Git. He ran up the steps grabbed the puppies dropped them down off the porch and placed the coat back over Thomas Pittman's head pausing looking at the face. Thomas Pittman's eyes and mouth were open.

The puppies' mother Trader came slowly from around the corner of the house followed by three more puppies. The porch puppies went for her. She lay on her side in the shade of the eaves over little holes made by rain dripping from the roof and gave milk tiny puppy-mouth hairs touching her nipples tongues and mouths making tight sucking noises.

That afternoon late Thomas Pittman was laid out somewhere in the house. Caroline and Walker decided that his heart burst. Caroline had come upon him she told people lying face down in a cotton row.

That night Walker and his brother Julius sitting on the back steps smoking and talking decided to bury Thomas Pittman out beyond the kitchen beside the woods.

Word was taken by Ross to Mr Saunders to please lend two of his slaves to dig the grave at first light. From the back porch there was clear sight of them the next morning digging beyond the kitchen toward the woods. Their shirts were off and by the time the sun was on them they glistened.

Thomas Pittman was buried in a pine coffin made by Richard Stott. Richard let them use one he had made for his father who was lingering.

This is how the graveyard was started one summer. *Then in October, on the second full moon—that is, a blue moon—as the day died after sunset, but before dark, there gradually appeared the outline of Thomas Pittman rocking in a rocking chair beside his grave. And as he's been joined by others there in the graveyard beyond where the kitchen once stood, I, on blue moons, have seen and heard —still see and hear—them all.*

BLISS

At around lunchtime everybody started stopping work. I walked with Aunt Scrap over to the clearing between the graveyard and wisteria vine, where people were spreading blankets and quilts on the ground. Aunt Scrap took me into the edge of the woods and ran her rake softly across the pine straw. "See, you can still see where the cotton rows were." And there on the ground among the tall pine trees: gentle, undulating rows beneath the thick copper-colored pine straw.

Now that would have been something to give a report on in school.

Thatcher walked up. I grabbed his hand, which was rough from the work he'd been doing. Thatcher has very manly hands anyway. He works for Strong Pull Construction, and will eventually become a crane operator. It's been his lifelong dream.

Dan Braddock, sitting on the tailgate of Mr. Copeland's jeep truck, said to Aunt Scrap, who was getting food out of a basket in the truck bed, "Ain't it so, Aunt Scrap?"

"What's that?"

"About Hawk. Nigger woman nursing him and a pickaninny at the same time."

"Aunt Ricka, won't it? Some kin to that Zuba."

"I don't remember it," said Uncle Hawk.

"You ought to," said Mr. Copeland. He looked at me. I had just sat down on a blanket. "Hawk was so old before he stopped nursing, Mama told him if he'd just please stop, he could start smoking cigarettes."

Everybody laughed.

"Who was Zuba?" I asked Thatcher, who had just sat down beside me.

"Nigger man used to live on the place. He got hung with a stretch of wisteria vine for murdering a little girl. That same vine I reckon."

I was shocked to my toes.

Aunt Scrap handed me a ham-and-biscuit.

It was a joyous and merry occasion. The sun was bright through the lofty pines and we were in the cool shade drinking iced tea and eating lovely picnic food.

NORALEE

I like the graveyard. You can't step on the graves, but a dog gets on one and Aunt Scrap hollers.

Papa asks me if I can remember coming last year and I can. There is a little rock angel on Loretta's grave. Loretta was my grandma but I never saw her when she was alive. They talk about Loretta and the baby fingers. Then they talk about that rock pile and Meredith carries me down there on his shoulders.

Mr. Braddock talks about niggers. Mama says not to say nigger but everybody else does except Mama and Bliss.

Mr. Braddock is fat.

Then we eat.

Aunt Scrap has a surprise for me in her pocket. She always does. It's a piece of candy, but she says I can't eat it until after lunch. She hollers at Fox. Fox is Meredith's home dog. He's black and last time at the graveyard he licked some chocolate off my face.

Mark's home dog is Trader.

Mark wears a hunting knife and him and Meredith take me down to the rock pile where they see who can throw a great big white rock the farthest.

BLISS

At the rehearsal dinner, Uncle Hawk and Aunt Sybil sat across from Mother, Father, Thatcher, and me. I was a little concerned.

"What sort of work you into?" Uncle Hawk asked Father.

"Securities."

"Securities?"

"Right, securities."

"Is that in a bank or something?"

"No, not exactly. It's not in a bank."

"Some kind of paper work, though."

"You could say that."

"I never been in any paper work, course I hadn't wanted to either, but I imagine if I had, I wouldn't had the credentials to do that sort of thing. I'm too tan, too."

"Hum," said Father, chewing on his steak. The dinner was absolutely wonderful. Thatcher and I held hands under the table.

"What sort of work do you do?" Father asked.

"Transportation. Transportation and digestion is what I call it. I got a combination gas station, cafe, hardware-grocery store, and fruit stand. That's what I call it: transportation and digestion."

"That's right," said Father. "Bliss told me that—"

"Most people think that's right funny," said Uncle Hawk. He was leaning over his plate a little.

"It is funny," said Mother. But she didn't laugh.

And then, the most glorious day of my life.

The church was almost full for the wedding, both sides. On my side were all my aunts and uncles, a total of only four. Thatcher's family was there in full force, including Aunt Scrap.

My older sister, Claire, made it from Alabama and was my maid of honor, though we've never been close, and Mr. Copeland was the best man. Meredith and Mark were two of the ushers and were the handsomest little things in the world. Meredith had that twinkle in his eye throughout. He is so cute.

And yes, there's something of steel in Thatcher, in his eye and manner, that makes me know we'll be happy for the rest of our lives. I look forward to a full life as a wife and mother, friend and patient companion through the hardships one encounters along the pathways of life.

The reception took place in our backyard and I was upstairs putting on my trip suit when Mother walked in—apparently upset. "Who did you say the one with the red tie is?" she said.

"The one who sat across from us last night."

"That's Uncle Hawk. Thatcher's uncle. Mr. Copeland's brother—the one we went to see in Florida."

"Do you know what he's saying?" She put her fist on her hip.

"What?"

"Well, there's Ellie and Bob, and Dawn Harrison sitting around out there and he says, 'Yeah, I was working the roads in Albany, Georgia, in thirty-two and got fried chicken left beside a fence corner on one day, pork chops the next, and barbecue the next. By three women. Three different women. That's how organized I was.'

"And Ellie says, 'Why did they leave it beside a fence? Why didn't they just bring it to you?'

"'Cause I was working the roads,' he says.

"'What's that?' says Ellie, and Bliss, the man was on a chain gang!"

"I didn't know that."

"So then Larry Cain asks him how long he was on a chain gang and he says, 'Until I figured out I could get a file left for me just as easy as fried chicken.'"

"Well, Mother, he may have been exagger—"

"And then about a minute later he says he never shot but one man in his life, 'but he lived.'"

I didn't know what to say. What could I say?

"Well, don't you see how that sounds?" Mother says.

"No, not really, Mother."

"It's just not the kind of thing one wants to hear on one's daughter's wedding day." She was smoking a Pall Mall—red lipstick on the end. "And this Dan Braddock fellow—honestly," she said, blowing smoke.

55

"Now Mother, please," I said. "This is the happiest day of my life and I can't let something like that get in the way. Please."

Mother tends to find the least distinguished aspect of a situation and then focus on it for one to two hours.

MARK

Mother tells me the Scriptures are full of warnings about spilling your seed on the ground like Onan. Onan made God mad and God "slew him also." She says if God would do it then, He might do it now.

But I don't know what it means. She reads it to me when she catches me doing it. But I'm not going to do it anymore. But it's hard not to.

I do lots of good things to make up for doing it. I don't cuss like Meredith does, for one thing. We live next door to them and sometimes Mother comes and gets me if she hears him cussing. Last time she came out to the shop door and heard him.

Uncle Albert lets us play in the shop in the floatplane he's building. We bomb the Japs and the Germans.

While the people in the church are singing "Breathe On Me," I feel Jesus. Mother is singing in the choir. Meredith is

not here. He comes to Sunday school sometimes. Mother says
Uncle Albert and Aunt Mildred ought to make them all come,
and come themselves.

> Holy Spirit, breathe on me,
> My stubborn will subdue;
> Teach me in words of living flame
> What Christ would have me do.
> Breathe on me, breathe on me,
> Holy Spirit, breathe on me;
> Take thou my heart, cleanse every part,
> Holy Spirit, breathe on me.

Mr. Meacham walks down the aisle next to the far wall. His
head is bowed, and he's holding his handkerchief up to his face.
"Tarry not."
I look at my hands resting on the back of the wooden pew.
I feel Jesus pulling me down toward the preacher, down to
rededicate my life, whispering to me, moving in my feet. I
want to be true, clean, pure. I look up at Mother in the choir,
but the lights are in her glasses and I can't tell if she's looking
at me or not.
"All you have to do, friend, all you have to do is take that
one step, then let Jesus take your hand. Don't refuse him.
Don't hold back."
I let go. I step into the ocean, out into the aisle and watch
my feet walking, one and then the other, my brown shoes on
the thin, maroon rug—down past wooden pews in which I
used to sit with my head leaning over into the corner of the
pew, my ear picking up the hard echoes of all the people
singing loud, full hymns to God.

After the service people stand in line to shake my hand. Mrs. Boles, Mrs. Wood, Mrs. Toggart hug me. I smell their hair, dresses, perfume, and look into the sagging skin on their arms. I feel their breath in my ear as they whisper what a good boy I am. They're almost like aunts and uncles.

Mr. Bass, the preacher, asks the ones of us who have come down—me, two men, a red-headed woman, and another boy—to follow him back for a brief meditation. We walk through the door at the back of the auditorium, into the hallway which smells like wood and hymnals. I follow them through the junior department, where Meredith shot a broken paper clip at me with a rubber band one time while I was leading a song—and the clip stuck in my chin, and I kept on leading the song. After church I told on him.

We go into a classroom, sit, and the wicker chair-bottoms squeak.

"May we pray," says Mr. Bass.

I close my eyes and feel the church around me, the tall red brick walls, the white columns, the steps, the large rooms and smooth wooden benches. It feels good, like I'm where I'm supposed to be.

"Dear Lord," Mr. Bass prays, "be with us in our hour of need. Be with these who have sought Thee, have sought Thy healing presence, Thy love, oh Lord. We ask that Thou wilt bless them, grant each one the needs he has, Oh Lord, in Thy precious name, amen. Now if any of you would like to pray, please do."

The red-headed woman prays: "Dear Lord, Thou knows I whup little Judy Faye and it don't do no good. . . . Amen."

59

I see a little girl getting whipped over and over because she keeps doing mean things.

"Anyone else?"

Silence.

"Amen," says Mr. Bass. "Bless you all. I just wanted us to gather for a moment of quiet and prayer."

When we finish, Mother is waiting outside the classroom door.

Next day, Meredith and me sit in the floatplane frame on a bombing run over Germany.

I need to let him know. "Last night I rededicated my life to Christ."

"Why?"

"Because I had to. Jesus called me."

"You just want to be a goody-goody."

I am better than Meredith now, for sure. I was better than Meredith when he dropped those kittens down the well. I told him he was supposed to drown them in the pond but he didn't pay any attention. He just walks over to the well with the kittens in a potato sack and takes them out one at a time and drops them down the well by holding them right over the middle of the well, by the skin on their necks, turns loose, saying, "Bombs away." It goes sailing down to meet itself coming up in the picture, and splat hits, and the circles spread out in the middle, breaking up the blue sky. Three of the kittens hang onto the side until Meredith pours a bucket of water on them in a steady stream so that it pushes them out in the middle and they disappear. I was scared Jesus might come and get mad.

I was better than Meredith then, because he did it, and I didn't, and I'm better than he is now because I'm saved and rededicated and he's not either one.

"If you're not saved you'll burn in hell after you die," I tell him.

"I'm as good as you are."

"Not if you ain't saved."

"You don't know everything."

"I know that."

1959

THATCHER

Bliss and me moved in with Mama and Papa right after we got married. We're waiting for Mr. Sutton's son to move to Richmond, which he keeps putting off. Then we'll have a nice place to rent until we can save up for a down payment. Meredith has been the center of attention lately, as usual. First off, he got in trouble at school because he got the address of this group from Miami and he wrote a letter saying he had fifty volunteers ready to go fight Castro and they wrote him a letter back saying that American citizens couldn't fight down there, but that they appreciated his interest.

I wish they'd sent about ten combat trucks to the school and said, *Okay, boys, let's load 'em up.*

Mrs. Bingham got aholt of the letter and gave it to Mr. Temple and he called in Meredith and asked him what was going on. Meredith said he was ready to go fight, but that it was Mark's idea to write the letter. Mr. Temple called in Mark and Mark said he knew about it, but it won't his idea. Then

Mark told Aunt Esther and she complained to Mama.

Papa found out and told Meredith he couldn't go out to the shop for a week. Papa is still working on that floatplane out there—off and on. Meredith got the picture of the finished product out of the instructions and stuck it on his wall, which don't make much difference because Papa don't seem to be too interested in the instructions anyway. He's more interested in the notebook. He's supposed to keep that in case the thing crashes, I reckon. Then they can look in there and see why. He finally got both engines started at the lake but nobody wouldn't ride with him so it was whopsided in the water until he moved over in the middle. Then he drove it around on the water again. But he wrote it up wrong. He had the temperature, wind direction, and all that in here, and then in the narrative account he says, "First successful in-air operation today. Aircraft lifted into air on eight separate occasions." What happened was he run it across this speed boat wake twice and it bounced eight times. I told him that didn't count but he wouldn't talk about it.

Now he's putting family trees in there.

Anyway, Meredith and Mark are always going out there sitting in it and pretending they're flying. It's going to be made mostly out of aluminum and tight canvas. One problem is that some of the kit is missing, which Papa says is okay because he can tell from the parts already there how to make the missing parts.

So now Meredith can't go out there and sit in the frame for a week because he got called to the principal's office.

I swear, Meredith.

I seen this thing with him and the well coming. If you told

66

me somebody was going to fall down the well—the open well under the rotten spot in the kitchen floor—I could have told you it would be Meredith. Anybody could—from the way he pushed on the spot all the time. To make it creak. It creaked like a little moan. Day or night, he'd be standing over there pushing down with his foot, making them noises.

He came in, pushed on the floor one time too many and there he goes like a rope had jerked him straight down through the floor, turning his head to look at me—his face following his shoulders on down through the floor, and down into the well. Swallowed up.

Served him right.

We abandoned that well six, eight years ago because he threw a litter of kittens down it. Papa told him to put them in a potato sack and drown them in the pond, but oh no, not Meredith. Too much trouble. So he just drops them down the well, one at a time. Then Mama comes along, pulls up the well bucket and there's a drowned kitten in there—looks like a soggy black sock—and I bet you could have heard her scream a mile away. She swore off cooking with that water and said there was no choice but to dig a new well and put in regular plumbing. Everybody else had regular plumbing and it was time we had it too, she said. Papa said plumbing won't nothing but a passing fad. And Mama wanted a new kitchen added on to the house over the old well.

So anyway, Papa got a new well dug, tore down the old well shed, covered the hole, and built the new kitchen over that hole.

The problem of the floor getting rotten was because of several things. For one, the joists were four instead of two feet apart. Mr. Hoover told Papa about that but he didn't pay no mind. Another thing was that the kitchen had about a five degree slant down toward the backyard, so that if something leaked, like the sink or refrigerator, the water ran to a spot in the floor which happened to be right over that open well.

Meredith had this game with marbles and a glass. He'd turn a marble loose up at the high end of the floor and let it roll down toward a turned-over glass—one of those colored aluminum glasses that get real cold when you put ice in them —the kind with the turned-out lip. The marble would go right up in there. Meredith wouldn't play except when Papa was home.

Then there was this post stuck in the middle of the floor. It was supposed to be there for support, but it was nailed about a foot off the nearest joist and didn't support nothing.

Another problem was that Meredith kept crawling up under the kitchen, throwing things down the well, and leaving the top off—which made the floor damp right in front of the refrigerator. See, Meredith was using that well as a place to get rid of things, and if it was alive he'd shine the flashlight down there and watch it drown.

So the dampness coming up from the well, and the fact that people stood right there in front of the refrigerator a lot, sort of suspended between those far-apart joists, and the fact that the sink and refrigerator leaked—all this worked together, and that place in the floor got to be like the soft spot on a baby's head, and Meredith just couldn't get enough of making it creak and moan.

On the night it happened, two, three weeks ago, I'm standing at the kitchen sink washing arrowheads. Mama, Bliss, Meredith, and Noralee are in the living room watching "I've Got a Secret."

Papa has his teeth out, which makes him lisp. "Thun," he says, "go get me thum buttermilk." Mama hates it when he talks with his teeth out.

Well, Meredith mumbles something, then comes on back. He's in his pajamas. And while he opens the refrigerator door, he pushes down with his bare foot on the rotten spot, just to make it groan. Then he gets the buttermilk, steps back on the rotten spot, and the floor, all of a sudden, sort of crunches open with a loud crack and there he goes—turning his face to look at me with this "Lord, it did it" look; there he goes right on out of sight *still holding on to that jar of buttermilk.*

You hear this deep splash, with a kind of a bathtub-bottled sound.

I stood there. I was in no hurry.

Papa, Mama, Bliss, and Noralee come running in and Papa bends over the hole and yells, "You down there?"

"Where you think I'm at?" The echo hangs in the well.

Then there's this little splashing around, like he's moving. I walk on over to the hole.

"Joists were too far apart," I said to Papa.

"I could have told you them joists were too far apart," Meredith yells up.

Mama stood up straight, looked at Papa, and then bent back over the hole. She was scared. And Bliss was scared. I could tell by the way she looked. Didn't scare me. I knew Meredith was too hard-headed to get hurt falling down a well.

Papa says, "We uth to keep thoup down the well—dropped it down in a clean bucket with cheeth cloth acroth the top."

Bliss looked at me like "do something," but I figured it'd work out. Just give it a little time.

Papa told me to get the flashlight, but I couldn't find it, so he struck a match, got on his knees, and reached down into the well with the match as far as he could. Didn't do no good.

"I'm going to shinny up," yells Meredith.

"Wait till we find the flashlight," says Bliss.

"I don't need no flashlight."

About then Papa found the flashlight in the pantry, came back, shined it down the well, and we all saw Meredith. He was coming up, pushing with his hands and knees against the well casing—one hand, one knee, the other hand, the other knee. Down below him you could see the dark water reflecting the flashlight. And his pajamas, the blue ones, printed with the crossed rifles, were all wet and stuck to his shoulders—the wet making the skin show through. He wears that same pajama top to baseball practice.

"Wait a minute and we'll throw you a rope," says Papa.

"Never mind," says Meredith, grunting. "I can make it like this."

"Whereth a rope?" says Papa, looking around, still shining the light down on Meredith.

Meredith looks up at us and his face is all splotchy white and red, and he tells Papa to turn off the flashlight because he can't see how far he is from the top. So Papa clicks off the flashlight and lays it down and that flashlight just slowly rolls right into that black hole before anybody can grab it and when it hit Meredith it sounded solid, like a hammer hitting a tree—got him right on the head. Then there is this heavy, scratchy scrambling followed by a short silence, then this loud, deep splash.

Meredith goes through his teeth: "What the hell was that?"

"The flathlight. Can you uth it?"

"You dropped the flashlight?"

"Look around. It'th suppoth to float."

"Meredith cussed," said Noralee. "You're not supposed to cuss in the house," she says down to Meredith.

"I ain't in the house. I'm in the well."

Mama tells Bliss to go call the fire department and I could tell they were both worried. Papa said we didn't need no fire department, and then he remembered the rope under the front seat of the truck and told me to go get it. I told him that rope was only five or six feet long. Meredith was a good twenty-five feet down.

But Papa gets this idea: add sheets onto the rope. So I went out to the truck, got the rope, came back, and Mama had collected a few sheets from the beds. Bliss had called the fire department.

In a minute, Bliss and Papa were passing these tied-together sheets, one at a time, down into the well. About the time the sheets were out of sight and just the rope was left above the floor, Meredith yells up, "Okay, tie that end to something. I've got aholt to this end."

Well, we look around for something to tie the rope to.

The post.

Papa gets positioned on the side of the post away from the well, wraps the rope around the post, ties it into a knot, braces his foot against the post, and wraps what's left of the rope around his hand. I had my doubts, but I didn't say anything.

Noralee, who's standing there with her arm stuck between her legs she's got to go to the bathroom so bad, says, "What if that post comes loose?"

"Mr. Hoover said that post won't put in solid," says Mama.

"Poth ain't coming looth," says Papa. "Joe Ray Hoover don't know everything. He thirtenly never built bridgeth in the war." Papa does his jaw motion. He has this habit of—with his teeth out—bringing his lower jaw right up under his nose, in this chewing motion, so that the whole bottom half of his face disappears up into the upper half. And he needed a shave.

"It could come loose," says Noralee.

Papa don't pay her no mind at all. He just yells down to Meredith, "All right, climb on up."

"You got that end tied to that post?" Meredith wants to know.

"The rope is thanchioned, Meredith," says Papa. "Climb on up."

"It's what?"

"Thanchioned."

"What?"

I didn't know what it meant either.

"Thanchioned! Thanchioned! Now climb on up like I told you!"

The rope tightened and squeaked on the post—which held. It held for a right good while, as a matter of fact, until Meredith was about halfway up, and then it snapped free real loud there at the bottom, jerked the rope out of Papa's hand, shot to the hole and wedged there. The damn knot held. And Meredith held on to the sheets. I guess he dropped about five feet. Papa can tie a knot. I'll say that.

"What happened?" Meredith yells up, shaky.

Papa says, "Nothing. Keep climbing." He hadn't no more than got the words out of his mouth when this little bitty rip starts somewhere in one of them sheets, sort of speeds up, then goes real fast, and there goes old Meredith again. Right back where he started from. Another loud, bottled splash sound.

Noralee says, "He ain't gonna ever get out of there."

Mama turns on Papa. "Albert, this kitchen has gone all this time rotting through, and you messing with them rabbit boxes and airplane plans. How do you expect to build an airplane if you can't build a kitchen? And now something like this happens. This floor ought not to ever got like this in the first place. Joe Ray Hoover told you about this kitchen."

Papa's mouth dropped open and his eyes darted around all over Mama's face. Then he did his jaw motion, turned, and walked out the back door.

"Papa, I could of told you that post would pop out," Meredith yelled up.

"He ain't up here, Meredith," I said.

The fire truck drove up. We could hear the loud idle of the engine. The fireman hit the siren for a low growl.

"We don't need no fire truck," said Meredith.

I walked out onto the back doorsteps and saw the firetruck headlights shining on Papa, sitting on the ground beside the well house, spotlighted, his head in his hands. The firemen, a tall one and a short one, walked up to him. Papa pointed to the kitchen, and they came on in and dropped the rope ladder down the well, hooked the end to the well curb, and in a

73

minute out climbed Meredith, his pajamas dripping water. A red bump was on his hairline in front. Served him right.

Bliss thinks there is no end to his cuteness.

"Where's Papa?" he said.

"He's out in the backyard," I said.

Mama says, "Go on to the bathroom, Noralee." Then she went to get a towel for Meredith.

"Y'all didn't have to come," says Meredith to the firemen. "I could have got out."

"Then jump back down there and climb out," I said.

He gave me his go-to-hell look, then followed the firemen out. He stood on the back doorsteps. Me and Bliss stood on the porch. Papa was still out in the yard.

"What do we owe you?" Papa said to the firemen.

"Not a thing."

"What about that 'natural suspension,' Papa?" said Meredith. "In the kitchen floor?"

Papa walked over to the base of the steps. Meredith was on the second step. The backdoor light shined in Papa's eyes. "Don't talk to me about 'natural thuthpension' becauthe you don't know what you're talking about. You don't know nothing about building bridgeth, and Joe Ray Hoover don't neither.

"Why don't you write *this* up in the notebook?" I said.

"I ain't studying no notebook," he said, sort of digging his hand down in his overall pocket.

"Go put your teeth in," says Mama.

THE VINE

The leg belonged to Timothy Cook who worked at the mill.

Timothy's mother Delphi came the morning after the explosion and sitting in her buggy talked first to Caroline. I just don't feel right about burying his leg in the same graveyard with Thadeus you know at the same time and all she said. It just don't seem right somehow. And that's such a nice little graveyard out there.

It's fine with us I'm sure said Caroline.

I favor a small ceremony. Timothy of course won't be able to come. If I could just get a body to holp me a bit.

We will Mrs Cook. One of us. Where is the leg now?

Well they brought it wropped up and put it in our smokehouse. It's from his knee down. It's just awful but gracious sakes it can't stay out there.

We'll send Ross after it and build a box for it. Then after supper about sundown we'll have a little service. You come on over and bring whoever you want to.

Walker came up.

We're going to bury Timothy's leg out here in our graveyard said Caroline.

Leg?

Why sure. It'll give him great pain if we don't dispose of it
rightly.

Well we got room.

I'd be mighty obliged said Mrs Cook. It is a nice little
graveyard with the babies and all and I want to dispose of
his leg rightly. I told him what I had in mind and he seemed
agreeable. I certainly appreciate it. She drove away in her
buggy.

A few minutes later Walker said to Ross You need to build a
coffin for Timothy Cook's leg. Then you'll have to go get the
leg. It's in their smokehouse. We're going to bury it out here
this evening.

A coffin?

A coffin. A leg coffin.

I got to go get his leg.

That's right.

How much of it got blowed off?

It was at his knee. Make it a infant coffin like the others. A
little longer maybe. Walker held his hands showing the length.
That'll be plenty long. No need for nothing fancy. And the
grave needn't be deep. I'll dig it.

That evening they stood in a small group out in the graveyard read a Bible scripture and buried the leg.

૨૦

On the next blue moon, the leg was in a dark maple rocking cradle, just like the cradles for three infant cousins of the family who were out there with Thomas Pittman, and were crying. Thomas Pittman couldn't see the leg in the coffin because it was added at the end of the short row of infants. But he sang to it along with the infants, even though they cried.

NORALEE

I know where home plate and first base and second base and third base is. I like third base best of all. Papa lets me play third-base coach sometimes because I'm a girl. I go with them down to the ball field when Papa takes us down there. Him and Meredith and Mark all pitch and hit. Thatcher used to come before he got married, but he'd just stand in the field way out there and scratch between his legs and look off at the woods and make Papa mad at him.

Papa gets mad at Meredith for not hitting the way he wants him to.

And Mark is the pitcher but Meredith wants to be.

The best thing that happened at the ball field was when Meredith slid the truck down the left field bank. Right down into the trash pile.

Meredith don't have his driver's license yet, but Papa lets him drive the truck down to the ball field and empty the trash over the left field bank where the trash pile is. Mark goes with him. Meredith don't ever let me go so I walk down there through the woods and watch them. He drives fast across the ball field and then the truck turns and slides around like everything. Sometimes they get out and throw rocks at jars or shoot the .22 at Pepsi bottles. And sometimes Meredith lets Mark drive the truck.

Papa don't know Mark goes down there with Meredith. I'm waiting to tell on them when either one tells on me about something.

Last winter it snowed real, real long and Meredith and Mark took the truck down to the ball field while everybody was gone off. The tires had chains but that didn't do no good.

I was in the living room when Meredith walked in the kitchen and said something to Papa. I walked to the door and listened.

"It's where?" said Papa.

"Down the left field bank at the ball field," said Meredith.

"In that trash-pile garbage dump?"

"Yessir."

"What the. . . . How. . . . Who did it?"

"Mark."

They walked out the back door and I got my coat and boots and followed them. Papa slipped on the ice and Meredith grabbed him.

We stepped into the screened-in porch at Mark's house and stomped our feet. The porch was quiet and dark because of the deep snow on the ground and the snow stuck in the screen.

Aunt Esther opened the door. I smelled meat loaf. "Wait a minute," she said. "Let me get you a broom to clean off them shoes with." Mark came up behind her.

She handed out a broom and closed the door.

Papa told Aunt Esther what happened and she got mad at Mark. Then Papa, Meredith, and Mark walked to the ball field. I followed them. I walked on top of the glaze on the snow.

When we got there it was getting cold. Their faces were red in the cold. They looked down at the jeep. It was pointed uphill. The whole weather seemed like it was gray.

"One of your earflaps is up," said Meredith to Papa. Papa was wearing his old hunting cap with the earflaps.

"That ear ain't cold."

Meredith looked down at the truck. "We'll get it out," he said. "And we can come down here and start it up every morning until the snow goes away."

"It really ain't so bad," said Mark.

They stood looking down at the truck.

"I swear," said Papa. "My jeep. In the trash pile."

"It didn't quite reach the trash pile," said Meredith.

They started walking home. I followed them. I stayed on top of the snow but they sunk in.

Meredith stopped at a place where a shortcut turned through the woods. Papa was in front and kept walking. I was behind. Mark kept walking behind Papa, crunching in the snow, then stopped. I stopped. Papa kept walking. Meredith nodded toward the woods and him and Mark went that way.

I caught up with Papa and stayed close behind him because I didn't know what they might be getting ready to do in the woods.

THATCHER

Why the hell do I have to get the damn truck out of the damn trash pile? Why me? It don't make sense. If I had drove the damn truck over the damn left field bank of the ball field you think *Meredith* would be helping get it out? Hell no. You think Papa would make him help get it out? Hell no. You think Meredith would be within twenty miles when I got it out? Hell no. You think it would make any difference to Papa where Meredith was when I was getting the truck out if I drove it down there? Hell no.

Papa wouldn't even ever let me drive hardly. And that's after I got a driver's license. And Meredith don't even have a driver's license yet because he didn't pass driver's education. He got a note sent home because he told Sandra Tilly, right before her time to drive, when they walked around the car trading places, that she would have to slam on the brakes because they were real weak and went all the way to the floor, but the brakes really had just been serviced and tightened—feather sensitive—and Sandra Tilly hit the brakes like stomping a snake I reckon and went into a skid which scared her so bad she had to drop out. The next note said Meredith was out of driver's training because he had run off the road trying to run over a possum that somebody had hit and not killed. And driver's training was run by Coach Kelly, who wouldn't get upset at just anything. And another thing is Meredith and Mark both got kicked off the ball team for two weeks because Meredith stuck a record needle in the seam on a baseball at one of their ballgames so that when Mark pitched it it would jump all around. Nobody had ever heard of doing it except Mark read it somewhere and of course Meredith had to try it out. If it can be tried out, Meredith will try it out.

So we borrow Babe Terrell's tractor, that off brand Earth-Master, made in Russia or somewhere, which has strange gears I ain't used to—but I can drive the thing. Papa borrowed Fred Burgess's John Deere. See, it was Papa's idea to pull the truck out with two tractors.

The snow melted, and on a Friday night before we pulled it out Saturday, he sat us all down in the living room. At night he'll sit us on the couch instead of outside on the root.

"Okay," he said. "I'm going to explain to y'all how we're going to get the truck out of the trash pile. With a little thinking and a little natural suspension you can do almost anything. Physics. Now the angle up that bank is high enough that the friction available to the tires of one tractor probably ain't going to do it. Friction is how one surface holds another, and the earth on the left field bank has to hold the tractor wheels or they'll spin. If they spin the truck stays where it is. With two tractors there'll be half as much chance of each one spinning so you're working on the principal of friction in your favor. What natural suspension does is—"

"Why don't you get a wrecker down there and wrench it out?" asked Meredith.

"Because with two tractors you can get at natural suspension. Be quiet."

"Why ain't Meredith getting it out?" asked Noralee.

"He is. He's helping."

"That's a good question," I said. "He's getting helped by the whole neighborhood. I'd hate to see what would have happened if it'd been me drove the truck down the left field bank."

"I didn't drive it down there," Meredith said. "Mark did. But it was both of us in there. Both of us'll have to pay." ʼ

"Pay what?" I asked.

"Whatever it costs."

"That's a joke. It ain't going to cost nothing."

"If we get a wrecker."

I got the EarthMaster and drove it down to the ball field Saturday afternoon. Mr. Thompson, the principal, had found out about it and he was down there. And Bliss, and Papa, and about ninety kids.

We hooked up two long chains to the front axle of the truck. Papa had Mr. Burgess's John Deere. I said why don't we try it with one first, and Papa said that would be like wasting food, that we had two tractors and we ought to use them both, and you couldn't get at natural suspension with just one tractor. Just like Papa.

Mr. Thompson made all the kids stand back fifty feet in

case a chain link popped, which it won't about to do. The truck pulled right up, easy. One tractor could have done it. But there was some kind of metal box from the trash pile that had jammed up under the truck while we were pulling it out so we had to jack it up and get that out. Mr. Thompson made all the kids stand back again, said the truck might fall. Hell, the kids probably wished they hadn't bothered to come.

So before I drove Babe Terrell's tractor back, I told Meredith that I was going to pay Mr. Terrell a dollar for gas and would he please fork it over since he was paying for the rescue. He says he don't have a dollar and Mark forks out a dollar and Meredith says he'll pay him back half. So I told Papa that so far Mark had paid one dollar on expenses and Mr. Meredith had not paid one red cent, which on doomsday still won't be paid.

PART TWO

1967–1968

1967

BLISS

We left as usual at four a.m. last Thursday morning for our Florida trip, my tenth. This year the trip had a somewhat different flavor because of two reasons. First, and most dreadfully, Meredith and Mark will both be leaving for military service next summer—Mark for pilot training and Meredith, the Marines. While this was not discussed at great length, and I'm confident will not be, I couldn't help letting my dread and heartbreak slip into casual conversation. Meredith and Mark are, of course, enthusiastic about their upcoming "adventures"—as they see them. There is nothing I can do to abate their eagerness.

The family doesn't seem to be particularly bothered, or perhaps I mean they don't show it.

The second reason the trip had a somewhat different flavor was the presence of Meredith's fiancée, Rhonda Gibbs, a young blond woman of strong personality, heavy makeup, hoarse voice, with nonetheless a good heart, I'm sure. She sings in a rock-and-roll band. Meredith has dated her off and on for a long time, but their relationship has really taken off since summer. He's kept me posted, and got me to help him pick out a diamond ring which he gave her at Thanksgiving. They've yet to settle on a wedding date, however.

Meredith has changed so little since Thatcher and I got married it's almost a miracle. It's as if little Meredith, with his cocky walk and that ever-present twinkle in his eye, suddenly became *grown* Meredith with that cocky walk and ever present twinkle in his eye. He hasn't calmed down one bit. He's working for General Telephone, a lineman, and loves it. I so tried to get him to go back to Listre Community College. He went for one year and then dropped out. Though his grades didn't show it, he's certainly smart enough to go to college. When I talk to him about it, he always says he wants to work outdoors with his hands, then he'll say what Mr. Copeland is always saying: "There's no tool like your fingers."

Meredith and Mark have remained good friends—hunting and double-dating together in spite of the fact that Mark has entered, and next spring will graduate from, East Carolina College, though they aren't as close as they were when they were younger. Lord knows what all Meredith has gotten Mark into in their brief lives. The most recent discovery was that a year or two before Meredith fell down the well, he and Mark dropped a tombstone and a chicken down there. Somebody told that story at the last gravecleaning.

The last ten years have flown by. I got a secretarial position at Listre Elementary after two years at Listre Community College, and we saved most of my salary. Then after four years of that, our precious son, Taylor, was born—Taylor Meredith.

He's four now, looks like both of us, and has a very sweet disposition. Since he was born I've been working part-time at the school. Thatcher's been promoted to crane operator at Strong Pull. He's very good and has turned down two offers of an administrative position, though he's decided to take one next time they offer it. He's exempt from the draft because of his age and also because of Taylor, thank goodness. Meredith calls Thatcher "the crane pain."

But anyway, in one car were Taylor, Noralee, Mr. Copeland, Mildred, and Miss Esther. Noralee, thank goodness, loves to take care of Taylor. And in the other car were Thatcher, Meredith, Mark, Rhonda, and me—Thatcher driving.

One of the first things that happened, before light, was Rhonda started making up a song—about the floatplane —and got the rest of us in on it.

Mr. Copeland stopped taking the floatplane to the lake after the first year or so, then started back, then stopped, but he's kept tinkering with it off and on in the shop. He filled up one notebook about it, and now has started on a second one.

We called the song "The Floatplane Blues."

I got the floatplane blues, swimming round my head;
I got the floatplane blues, swimming round my head;
I want to fly with the eagles, but
I float with the frogs instead.

And so on.

Rhonda has a rare combination of loudness and softness not often found in a single human being. And the perfect name for herself. Rhonda. Meredith is crazy about her and I think they will probably be good for each other though I hope they wait until he's out of service before they get married.

Rhonda's family moved into the Jenkins' house beyond the field across the road when Rhonda was about six or seven —and Meredith was, I guess, ten or eleven. They would talk at the school bus stop. Then he took her fishing, of all things. She'd tag along when Meredith and Thatcher or Mark, or all three of them, went. Then she started "coming out" and there was Meredith, ready to love.

Meredith told me about something that happened one day right after he graduated. He's always been good about talking over things with me. The secret is: I listen. He comes to me. Anyway, he said that she took him into the barn over there close to her house to show him some kittens and what happened was—and I can just see the shaft of light coming in through the cracked barn door, hay dust in the air—what happened was, there's Rhonda in the corner on her knees, picking up a kitten and saying how she likes to feel them against her breasts, which she all but exposes by unbuttoning her blouse and pressing the innocent kitten to them while Meredith stands with the shaft of light behind him—bearing in to beat upon the barn floor. He told me he didn't know what to do, and so he left. But I'm not so sure. Meredith does not, in general, seem timid around women. It's an interesting question about Meredith.

But what I also know is that at some point after that Rhonda took *Mark* skinny-dipping. Mark alluded to it, but I never got the straight of it. I don't know if Meredith ever found out or not.

What happened on the trip down this time—besides

singing—was that Thatcher started telling stories to Rhonda about Meredith and Mark, stories Rhonda hadn't heard, and some I'd never heard either. It was great fun, joyous even —though this was all in the face of Meredith and Mark leaving—and as we zipped along through South Carolina we were all feeling relaxed and happy, and Thatcher told the story about the truck in the pond.

THATCHER

I was going bass fishing. I heard them when I got down to the graveyard. They had the ski rope hooked to the back bumper of the truck. Mark was in the water about fifteen feet from shore, wearing a orange life vest, holding on to a handle at the end of the rope. Meredith was behind the steering wheel in the truck, up on the dam, holding his arm high out the window, racing the engine. He dropped his arm, popped the clutch, and that old truck started out—along the car path across the dam part there at the deep end of the pond. The back end of the truck swerved, and up comes Mark, skiing. I couldn't imagine it all going so smooth, so I just decided I'd watch through the wisteria vine.

Meredith drives the truck into the pond on Mark's second or third time skiing. He was looking out the window, back over his shoulder at Mark, gas pedal on the floorboard it sounded like, when the truck left the car path. He looked back ahead to see where he was going, slammed on brakes

—too late. The truck slid—all four wheels locked, sending up dust—nose first, down toward the water, splashed in and floated away from the bank like some kind of odd boat—like the floatplane. The engine choked off. Mark skied right past the truck and straight into the dam. At first I was just going to stand there and watch. I mean, I can see the sunlight reflecting off the chrome around the windshield, and everything all of a sudden real quiet. Meredith is sitting in the cab with the window down, his elbow on the window sill, not moving—like he had just pulled into a gas station. Then he said something, and looked down in the floorboard. I was too far away to hear.

Great big bubbles start to belch up around the truck. It starts sinking, tilting forward fast.

I come out from behind the vine. "Get out, Meredith!" I say. "It's sinking! Get out!"

Water is halfway up the door. I start running down the bank as fast as I can, getting shed of my shoes and pants. I dive in and start swimming as fast as I can with my head out, watching. He opens the door. Water swirls through the crack, pushing the door back against him. Water is up to the window bottom.

"Come out through the window!" I yell.

He turns his face and chest upward, and starts sliding out through the open window with his hands on top of the cab. Then the water covers up his head. The cab is almost out of sight—you can only see the flat top, at water level. Meredith's hands sort of grabbed across the top of the cab at the same time water moved over it, kind of like a wave running over a sandy beach. I had *finally* got there. I grabbed at him, found an elbow. He surfaces, hits me in the chin with the top of his head, and scrambles up onto the top of the truck, which was about a foot under water. He kneeled on his hands and knees as the cab sunk on down, and said, right in my face, "I had to wait." His hair was flat and shiny, water dripping from his nose. "Did you see how I waited?" He stood on the cab, waved his arms to keep his balance, fell backwards into the water and then swam to shore. I swam behind him.

We sat on the bank, breathing hard.

"I didn't think you'd ever get out of there," Mark said.

"What took you so long?" I said.

He looked at me. "What?"

"What took you so long?"

Then he slapped me across the side of my head with his open hand. Little Meredith. It stung and made me deaf in that ear for a minute. He stood and started walking toward home.

I stood up and followed him, grabbed him and turned him around. I couldn't figure it. He knew I could bust his ass. "What did you do that for, Meredith? What the hell did you do that for?" Something had snapped in his head or something.

"Why did you ask me about taking so long?" Then he screamed, "What did you ask me that for?" His fists were balled up, his chin sticking out.

"What are you talking about?"

"Don't you see, goddamn it to hell? You damn shit. That's what Papa would ask if I almost drowned. 'What took you so long? What took you so long?'" Then he screamed in my face: "'What took you tho long?' I almost drowned, Thatcher."

96

Hell, I left him alone and let him walk on up to the house. It was crazy. He just went out of his head. The damn truck was in so deep you couldn't even see any part of it. We had to find it with a long pole. Papa got it all figured out how to get out, of course. Came up with the idea of being a frogman again. A wild idea. But it worked. I give Papa that much credit.

We needed a bulldozer. My foreman asked Mr. Durham if we could use one of Strong Pull's and he said yes, if we could get the newspaper to cover it. I'd just started working for Strong Pull Construction.

So we got the newspaper to cover it. Papa walked in the pond with a cinderblock tied around his ankle and the water hose in his mouth so he could breathe and hooked a chain around the rear axle of the truck. Then I pulled it up out of the pond with the bulldozer. Papa saved the damn newspaper clipping and the last time I looked it was stuck in the notebook—the floatplane notebook, the new one he's started.

THE VINE

Caroline came onto the back porch holding the bundle. She came on out and down the steps. She was wet to her elbows and her face was red and full of worry and her hair around both ears was matted red and wet from listening against the baby's chest. She walked across the yard to the kitchen and laid out the baby on a chair just inside the kitchen door. Mrs Saunders's slave woman Easter who was helping out came onto the back porch saying She's getting up Miss Caroline. She's getting up.

Caroline met Vera on the porch.

Vera was the color of hay. I want to see it Mama.

Don't make no difference honey. He was just born dead. No heartbeat at all. It happens. It just happens. You need to lay down.

I want to see it that's all said Vera. She held to Caroline's shoulder. Let me lean on you.

On the way back into the house Vera said I want him

buried out there with the field hand and the others.

That'll be a good spot. It's pretty out there.

Oh Mama. Vera stopped in the yard. When I wrote Seaton about Isaac he said we could

I know honey.

name him Isaac if it was a boy and then poor Seaton and now I can't even name him Seaton. There's not going to be a Seaton or a Isaac in the whole world.

Come on in and lie down now. You need to rest.

While the preacher prayed at the infant's graveside little Jenny Carmichael came running around the side of the house saw the ceremony in progress broke her run down to a fast walk and with red spots on her cheeks walked right on past the others up to Caroline whose head was bowed for the prayer. She pulled at Caroline's sleeve. Caroline opened her eyes and bent her head down to listen. Caroline broke ranks and walked sometimes skipping into a run past the house and out to the road. As they passed the porch little Jenny said Aunt Emma said you can see the head like a hairy fist coming out.

Late that afternoon Jenny told Ross how the baby boy had six fingers on each hand and how as Caroline cut off the two extras tiny stubby matchsticks tears were dropping off her nose and cheeks onto her hands and wrists.

Caroline brought the fingers home in a bottle of alcohol and put the bottle behind the clock on the mantle where it stayed and was talked about by the children until she and her grandson Tyree died of typhoid. Then Tyree's wife Loretta who wouldn't let her children wear bright colors on Sunday and who had always thought it obscene that the children climbed chairs and sneaked looks threw the little bottle with the fingers down the hole in the outhouse.

So then Thomas Pittman had another baby out there beside him. *They all appeared together on blue moon nights. Thomas in his rocker, facing the house, and four babies and a leg in rocking cradles made of dark maple. The new baby was quiet and still.*

Ross sat in the door to the smokehouse one rainy afternoon several weeks after the stillbirth and carved into the rock with a chisel BORN DED. On the next Sunday afternoon Vera called out to Caroline from where she stood beside the grave. Caroline walked out and stood beside her.

But it's spelled wrong said Vera.

He can spell it any way he wants to.

Well I'm going to ask him to do it over.

He worked a whole day on it and as far as I'm concerned he needn't waste time doing another one. Anybody knows what it says. Besides he lives here.

Vera pulled hair back out of her eyes. Why do you say that Mama?

It's true.

I know it's true. You don't like me living in town.

Caroline turned and faced the house. No I don't. Whoever heard of such a thing. Washing clothes with the niggers. It's not decent.

I do what I have to do to get along and I don't mind it.

Before Vera left that day she followed Ross out the back door into the yard. Ross will you change the spelling on the rock to dead D E A D.

It says dead. D E D.

Dead is D E A D.

It don't make no difference.

It does. It's my baby and I want it spelled right.

It's my rock. Do your own rock. It took me all day to do it.

Why don't you do your own rock? If you can get a rock in town.

Wouldn't harm you none to come to town Ross see some stores and factories.

We got stores around here.

I know it. You'd be surprised what all they got in town. It's not just fancy.

I been to town.

While Walker was away in the war a lone man dressed in a dusty blue uniform rode a horse into the backyard. He called out In here. A string of three wagons turned in and pulled up alongside the kitchen side of the house.

The family was in the fields.

The man went into the kitchen and came out with a blue plate of biscuits. He handed them around. There's probably some molasses another man said. He talked like the field hand. Another said Check the smokehouse. They got two hams from the smokehouse and put them into a wagon and then they drank directly from the well bucket without using the ladle.

They went back into the smokehouse and brought out a barrel of molasses and put that into the wagon.

Caroline and the family came back from the fields. Vera carried William who was Caroline's youngest in a basket. They stared at the men and passed slowly into the house. The soldiers paid them little mind. Caroline came back out to stand on the back porch for a few minutes looking at the soldiers. They sat around a fire they'd built in the yard. Then she walked by them to the kitchen. Their heads turned. One said something and a knot of about four of them laughed loudly.

Caroline came out of the back side of the kitchen and walked over to the smokehouse. She looked inside returned to the kitchen. In a little while she stood in the door to the kitchen a heavy cloth in each hand holding a pot of boiling water. She looked down to the ground and stepped out holding the heavy pot. The men were turning around to look at her as she approached the ones who had laughed. She said I wish you were red hot in the belly and in the middle of hell and heaved the water over them down onto their heads arms and necks. They scrambled screaming and one started for her grabbed her arm and pulled her sideways. She was still holding the pot in both hands as another said loudly Whoa watch out ducking behind a wagon wheel and pointing to the porch where Ross stood with a shotgun aimed at the soldier holding his mother.

Everyone moved slowly. The soldier turned Caroline loose.

Put that down lad said the one in charge. We'll not hurt your mother.

Put the gun down Ross said Caroline. These are thieves. They'll do anything. You shoot one you'll have to shoot them all and they'd git us sure. Put it down.

The one in command said to Caroline We're authorized to sustain ourselves.

There're ways to sustain without taking from women and children.

No ma'am there're not. Can you ask the lad to put his gun down?

Put the gun down Ross.

Ross lowered the gun slowly. His legs were shaking so badly he could hardly stand. Caroline walked to him took him by the arm and led him inside. Before dusk she came back out went to the kitchen and brought food back to the house.

Before eating their supper several soldiers walked to the graveyard and called to others who came and talked and laughed about Born ded. Bone did one said.

They left at sunup after Caroline and the children went to the field.

After the war Vera came home for good and Leon Herndon began to call on her. Walker Caroline Vera and Ross were at the corn crib shucking corn when he came the last time. William the youngest was lying in a small deep wagon on a quilt. It was late in the afternoon. Vera strode to Leon and together they sat on the front porch for a while. Suddenly Leon rode out of the yard and into the road still whipping the horse. The others at the corn crib stopped what they were doing and watched.

Vera stayed on the porch until much later when she went to the kitchen for supper.

That night deep in the night Walker came out onto the back steps for a smoke. Someone else got up inside went out onto the front porch then walked around the corner to the back steps. It was Vera. There was no moon but the sky was clear and the stars were out.

Papa is that you? You scared me.

What are you doing up?

I couldn't sleep. What are you doing up?

I wanted a smoke. I couldn't sleep either. Here. Here's some mosquito oil. Sit down. What did Leon want?

That's why I can't sleep. Vera rubbed oil on her hands then ankles forehead and neck. I keep seeing Seaton. I know Seaton died thinking of me. He said he'd be thinking of me if it happened and I can't rid myself of him. And I think about the baby dead out there with the field hand and those others. I don't want to rid myself of Seaton somehow but well Leon asked me to marry him and I said no I suppose.

You suppose?

I started talking about Seaton and he

You talked about Seaton when Leon asked you to marry him?

I mentioned how I felt and how I still think about Seaton. I don't blame Leon for driving off.

But Papa Seaton's there so strong.

Seaton's dead. You need marrying.

But I   That's why I can't sleep Papa. Vera started crying. She put her hands to her face and leaned forward so that her head touched her knees. The smoke from Walker's pipe hung above them in the darkness. Walker put his arm across Vera's back and drew her toward him. She put her head on his lap. He rubbed her back. They stayed that way for a long time before she sat back up wiping below her eyes with her hands. Walker pulled a handkerchief from his pocket and handed it to her. She spoke after sniffing her voice heavy from crying. Why can't you sleep Papa?

I just can't.

෧

A year later Bertha Finch was buried joining Thomas Pittman and the others in the graveyard. Bertha was Seaton's mother the grandmother of the stillborn infant and had often come from Raleigh to visit the infant's grave and decided that she too wanted to be buried in the country.

"... *and Walker told me too," said Thomas Pittman to Bertha Finch, "about picking up a hot coal one time, thinking it was a piece of chocolate. Julius, his brother, was standing there with him in front of the hearth, and had just kicked him or something about the time Walker saw what he thought was a piece of chocolate laying on the floor and picked it up. Well, you know, a piece of chocolate was a major occurrence. He picked it up and instead of yelling —now, remember it was hot—instead of yelling, he said, 'Julius, you want a piece of chocolate candy?' Julius says, 'Yes' and Walker hands it to him, and Julius has it on the way to his mouth before he realizes it's burning him like nobody's business. And it burnt him, burnt Julius, Walker said—brought a blister, but it didn't leave any sign at all on Walker. He used to tell that story every once in a while, and if Julius was around, Julius would show you the scar on his finger, then he'd try to kick Walker in the butt, and they'd do a little dance, trying to get at each other."*

"*They all did seem to be a right relaxed and hard-working bunch, and then Vera was so sweet on my Seaton.*"

"*I liked them a good bit. Oh, and them kids. What about Ross? He was always throwing rocks at chickens.*"

"*Ross was full of mischief. When Vera and Seaton were married he. . . .*"

BLISS

We stopped about once every hour to let the dogs out. We stop at the same side roads every year. It's a good way to notice how things change because every now and then a side road will be gone, with something built there, and we'll have to find a new side road.

We stopped in South Carolina just as the sun was coming up. We were on a side road of dark South Carolina soil—dirty sand. Mr. Copeland's car was a little ways up in front of us. Noralee was taking care of Taylor.

Thatcher and I leaned back against the front of the car, watching the edge of the blazing sun appear above distant trees.

"Do you suppose Meredith and Mark will be with us next year?" I said.

"I don't know. If they get leave."

Meredith and Mark were standing in the edge of the woods, watching the dogs. Meredith had a tennis ball he was throwing into the woods, and the dogs would fetch it. They are beautiful white pointers, with brown or black spots and freckles: Nick, Sam, Joe, and Sailor. Joe belongs to Mark and the rest are Mr. Copeland's.

"Well, I hope they'll have lots of leave time," I said.

"What?" said Noralee, walking up. She's fifteen, wearing glasses—in that awkward stage of puberty and gangly legs which will soon change into fluid beauty and grace.

"Meredith and Mark. I hope they'll be able to make the trip with us next year."

"I think it's stupid they're going in the first place."

"It's not stupid," said Thatcher. "How would you feel without the United States Army?"

"It would be all right with me," said Noralee.

"No, it wouldn't. That's stupid, Noralee. This day and age you don't have an army somebody will take you over."

"Not the Vietnamese," I said.

"Yeah, but you don't ever know. Nobody knew Hitler was such a big deal when he started out. You can't take the chance. You got to have a military arm."

"Why ain't you going then?" asked Noralee.

"You know why I ain't going. Taylor. And I'm too old."

"Load 'em up," called Mr. Copeland.

NORALEE

I love babies. I love to baby-sit. But I can't stand riding anywhere in the car with Papa. He reads all the signs out loud
for one thing and then when we stop somewhere he tries to
be cute with the waitress, and bores her to death.

These dogs get on my nerves, too. They sniff my crotch.
But Bliss lets Taylor ride with me and I love taking care of
him. He's real easy to get along with.

There's only one place so far that I won't go back to baby-
sit. The Parkers. They've got three children and their house
is the biggest mess I've ever seen and they don't even have
sheets on the beds. And they didn't pay me nothing hardly.

My favorite thing about Florida is Silver Springs. The rest
of it is b-o-r-i-n-g. It's just hunt, hunt, hunt, dead birds, dead
birds, dead birds. And the way they take their guts out and
everything is gross. The cats eat it.

We've got one teacher at school, Mr. Cresston, who talks
about Vietnam. But the principal called us in the auditorium

and told about being in Korea in the Marines and made a speech about what America stands for. I had Mr. Cresston's class right after that and he said there were two sides to the coin. Right before we left for vacation somebody said Mr. Cresston himself got called to the principal's office.

Meredith said he wanted to go in the Marines because it might be his only chance to get in a war and he didn't want to miss it. Mark wants to fly a jet.

What Papa would die if he knew about is J. W. Potts. J. W. is this black guy at school. He plays halfback on the football team and everybody loves him. He sat with me on the bus— I'm a cheerleader—on the last two road trips and he's really neat. The problem will come if he actually asks me for a date. I don't know what I'll do. I'll probably say no. But in a way I'd like to say yes because he's so neat.

We've got a game coming up at Grove City right after we get back and I've got to think up some stuff to talk about if he sits with me again.

One thing I like about him is he's a Christian and doesn't make a big deal out of it. He doesn't curse around me, but I've heard him curse, so a neat thing I told him about on the bus trip was Papa's "funk" speech to Meredith and Mark. I figured it'd be a neat thing to tell him, kind of bold, so I told him.

Papa had Meredith and Mark sitting out on the root one day. I was probably six or seven. I went out the front door instead of the back and then sneaked around the garage where they couldn't see me, came up on the far side, close enough to where I could hear. I thought all the time he was talking about "funking," but it was the other word. Papa don't always say his words clear. Later, when I told Bliss that I'd heard Papa explain about "funk," she spelled the real word and told me about it.

Papa was walking back and forth while he talked to Meredith and Mark. "When you start noticing animals doing it, it's time you know what to call it. Some people call it screwing, some call it having intercourse, capitating, making love, or funking"—I thought he said.

"Mark, your mama ain't likely to explain it to you. Our mama wouldn't ever mention about nothing like that. Now, your mama might talk *around* it once in a while when you're maybe forty or fifty."

"I already know about it," said Meredith.

I sat down and leaned my back against the garage. This was going to be interesting, I figured.

Papa told all this about his Papa telling him. Then he talked about peckers, about God giving all the male animals peckers and all the female animals snatches and that it was the best feeling thing in the world when you do it but if you did it to somebody you won't married to you could get a disease and your pecker might fall off. I remember wondering what might happen to my snatch.

I didn't tell it *all* to J. W., of course. I of course didn't say pecker or snatch. And I didn't tell him about Mama talking to me about having my period, which Tamantha Phillips's mother *forgot* to do.

When I told Bliss about it the first time, about Papa telling Meredith and Mark, I still thought it was "funk" because I'd never seen it written down then.

But Papa never set me down on the root and told me all

about it. I wish he would sometime. He set me down and talked to me about lying and cheating though.

The thing I ain't told J. W. about is how everybody in my family says "nigger" except Mama. I think he would understand it. He said he hears it at football games. We talked about that some on the bus.

THATCHER

Meredith had this little nigger buddy, City Lewis, that used to hang out at Bailey's Esso, and Meredith talked him into a basketball game one time, except instead of three or four guys, City recruited eight or nine.

They ended up down at the gym which was the old wooden gym they tore down two or three years ago. That gym wasn't hardly any bigger than the basketball court itself, and it had one bench up against the wall which went all the way around, and there was a big coal stove in the corner.

What was so weird about it was that there hadn't ever been any niggers in the gym except Pete the janitor and then suddenly one Saturday morning here was Meredith and Mark and Ted and Michael and Jerry and the nine niggers.

This was after me and Bliss were married because I remember asking Bliss if she wanted to ride down there with me to watch. She had something else to do.

They had built a fire in the coal stove in the corner and

were doing lay-ups when I got there. City and them had three cheerleaders dressed in green-and-white cheerleader outfits, with pom-poms, and they had some spectators along—two mothers who had driven them all down there, and four or five more. It was real cold, but I remember City had two or three players who were barefooted. He said they were the Tigers; what did Meredith's team want to be?

Meredith said the Floatplanes.

They started playing and the cheerleaders started cheering and their four reserve players lined up on the side. When a player got tired he'd get at the end of the line and the one at the front would go in the game.

I can't remember what the score was but it was real cold, I know that, so every time-out or break or something, somebody shoveled more coal into that stove.

The thing was that somebody had used the stovepipe as a target for coal bricks and dented it and knocked it out of kilter so that it leaked smoke where two sections of pipe fitted together. To fix it somebody would have to sit on somebody's shoulders and twist the loose section of pipe until it fitted tight. The game was about half over, the stove was red-hot, glowing, and smoke from the leak covered the ceiling—and was dropping lower and lower. The only light came from high-up windows and was turning a dark gold color.

Ted and Mike helped Mark up onto Meredith's shoulders and gave him a coat so that he could put his hands in the sleeves and not burn his hands on the pipe. He was going to fit the loose sections back tight so the leaking would stop. I'm just sitting there watching, waiting for the worse. I was at the back door, in case Mr. Thompson came in the front.

Mark had his hands in the sleeves like he was putting the jacket on backwards, up on Meredith's shoulders, the sleeves drooping over his hands. About the time Mark got hold of the pipe, Meredith touched his knee against the red-hot stove and jerked and hollered; Meredith lost his balance, and it looked like when you hold a baseball bat on the tips of your fingers but it falls anyway. Meredith tried to get back under him but it was too late.

When Mark fell he grabbed and took the whole pipe down with him. Only one section of pipe was left in the stove, and the black smoke roared out—like out of a train.

Everybody started doing different things then. Meredith got the shovel, knocked open the stove door and started shoveling out red-hot coals and throwing them out the gym door.

I stood up.

Black smoke was rolling down the back wall and the big black cloud was lowering. Meredith was dropping hot coals out of the shovel, onto the floor and Mark was kicking them out the door.

Somebody got a fire extinguisher from somewhere and started spraying in through the door on the hot coals. That made more smoke than ever come out the short pipe and the stove door.

You could see coal dust dropping from the air like it was sifting through somebody's hands. The bottom of the cloud was just about at everybody's heads and Meredith's face was as black as City's.

There was no choice but to leave. You couldn't see the goals. We just closed the door and left. I looked back at the gym, and smoke was seeping out through cracks in the boards and out the top corners of the door in two little black upward-flowing rivers, and sort of billowing out under the roof overhang.

But the worse part of the whole thing was that we walked to Mike's backyard to wash off our faces and Mrs. Tillman, their neighbor, saw it and told Mike's mother we'd been dressed up like niggers, and Mike's mother called Papa.

I was lucky, because I didn't go straight home, but Meredith and Mark did, and Papa met them in the yard, blessed them out for changing races, and told Meredith he was going to give him a whipping but he wouldn't say when. I think he waited about two weeks.

MARK

Meredith used to brag about getting Rhonda hot. We'd go frog-gigging and talk. One night, it's his turn to gig, my turn to row. Four bullfrogs are in the tow sack in the floor of the rowboat. Meredith sits in the bow, hands cupped over his mouth, answering a bullfrog. I'm in the stern, paddling toward the sound of the frog on the bank.

"Hurry up," he whispers over his shoulder. He picks up a three-pronged gig with one hand, a flashlight with his other hand.

I drag the paddle on one side and then the other, steering the boat toward the bellowing. Meredith stands slowly and hoists the gig like it's a spear.

The frog croaks from the bank straight off the bow. Meredith clicks on the flashlight, finds the frog sitting on the muddy bank just above water level, looking shiny wet, and sleepy. He holds the light on him and slowly extends the gig toward him as we approach the bank. Just before the boat touches land, he stabs the gig through the frog and into the mud. The frog croaks a muffled croak and kicks twice. Meredith gives the gig a quick swing up, lifting the frog into the air, lets the gig handle slide down through his hand, places the flashlight between his legs, almost loses his balance, pulls the frog from the gig, drops the gig into the boat, grabs the light and shines it on the frog, which he's holding for me to see. "He's a nice one. The biggest one yet," he says.

"Not as big as the last one."

"Bigger." He turns around, keeping his balance, picks up the tow sack and drops the frog in with the others. "Let's go fry some frog legs," he says.

"Yeah. I'm hungry."

Meredith balances the cast iron frying pan on two small logs at the edge of the fire and, with a stick, pushes several coals and small pieces of burning wood under it. He dips a spoon into a small jar of congealed bacon drippings, shakes it into the frying pan, wipes the spoon clean, unfolds a piece of waxed paper, spoons a mixture of cornmeal and flour from another small jar onto the waxed paper and rolls the washed frog legs in it until they are covered. He takes a pinch of flour and cornmeal between his thumb and finger and drops it into the pan. "It's not ready," he says. "I'm about to starve. You got that other stuff?"

"In the knapsack. Is it time?"

"Put it in that pan—the beans—and put it on the fire on the other side there, like I got this."

I get out a can of pork and beans, open them, pour them into a pan, and place the pan at the edge of the fire. Then I get out two deep red tomatoes, clean my hunting knife, and slice the tomatoes into a tin dish.

Meredith drops a pinch of flour and meal into the pan and it sizzles. "Thank goodness. Ain't you about to starve?"

"Yeah. I'm about to starve my ass off."

Meredith drops four legs into the grease. They sizzle. He rolls them several times. "Hand me that salt."

I hand the tin salt shaker to Meredith. He sprinkles salt as he rolls the frog legs in the pan, and talks. "They're going to be good. Just the right size. Not too big. Not too little. Papa won't do great big frogs. These are cooking just right, too. See that little bit of smoke coming up. That's just right."

"I know."

"If it's hot enough, and you get the flour to stick good, then they'll be real crisp. They're doing just right."

After they're cooked, we eat the frog legs along with beans and tomatoes on tin plates and drink water from our canteens. We eat slices of white bread with the meal, sop our plates with it.

"I wish we had some corn on the cob," said Meredith.

"Me too."

"The coals will be right in about fifteen minutes. What about old man Blackwelder's corn field?"

"Five minutes to get there," I say, "five to get the corn, and five to get back. The coals would be just right."

"Let's go. Get the flashlight."

"We don't need it. The moon's bright as day."

"Right. We don't need it."

The almost-full moon is so bright the clouds are white. We cross a field of broomstraw, a patch of woods, the road

—crouched and half running—and stop in a corn row. The stalks look black against the bright night sky.

When we get back, the campfire is a pile of smoldering, red-hot coals. A small flame flickers out, returns, another appears.

We push the corn ears up under the coals so they meet like spokes on a wheel, then cover them with hot coals, and sit watching.

"I wish we had some butter," I say.

"They're good with just salt. You don't need butter."

Later, Meredith takes a stick and spreads the coals away from two of the corn ears and rakes the ears onto the ground away from the coals. They steam, and are splotched with black where the coals have burned partly through the green shucks. "They look just right," says Meredith. "Let's see if this one's done. You'll burn your ass if you ain't careful."

He peels back the steaming-hot green and black shucks, jerking his hands away when he gets burned. He pulls away all the shucks, most of the silks, tosses the ear into the air and catches it, then quickly drops it, steaming, onto his plate.

"It smells sweet," I say.

"It's pretty, ain't it?" Meredith blows onto the ear of corn, sprinkles it with salt, bites into it, and chews, opening his mouth so he won't be burned. "Man, that's great. Taste that." He hands me the plate.

I take a bite. "Hummm. It's done—let's get the rest out."

"Pull it out and let it be cooling. Shuck that other one for you. This stuff is hot as Cora Gibbs's pussy," says Meredith.

I shuck the corn ear.

"You remember when Jack and Richard saw her and Bryan

Williams doing it in his car?" says Meredith. "Broad daylight?"

"Yeah, I remember that."

Meredith takes a bite of corn. "Hell, I got Rhonda hot. She gets hot real easy. She unbuttoned her blouse in the barn one time, too."

I don't talk about her doing that with me.

"They're all kind of wild or something," I say to Meredith.

"You ever had a girl to stick her tongue in your ear?"

"Sort of."

"'Sort of?'"

"Yeah."

"I'm talking about French kissing in your *ear*, not just plain old French kissing. There's a big difference. French kissing in your ear drives you crazy and if you do it in their ear it's guaranteed, double-d guaranteed to make them hot. You ever got a girl hot?"

"Of course."

"Who?"

"Christine Madrey."

"I thought so. Give me another ear. . . . I'm going to stick my tongue in it. Ha."

We eat three ears apiece and leave three for breakfast.

Late in the night, we crawl into the tent, under our blankets, and lie there.

"Let's see who can fart first," says Meredith. He farts.

We watch the dying coals.

"You ever hear about old Ross giving somebody a hot coal to eat?" says Meredith. "Told them it was chocolate?"

"Yeah, I heard that a bunch of times."

BLISS

On the first night things were the same as always. We watched television for a while, talked, the men fed the dogs, we went to our separate quarters.

Miss Esther and I were staying in Lee's room as usual —Uncle Hawk and Aunt Sybil's daughter who works in Kentucky. The same pictures were on the dresser: Lee's baby pictures, and Uncle Hawk in a uniform when he was very young, and Aunt Sybil and Uncle Hawk when they got married.

When we were getting dressed to go to bed I asked Miss Esther, "Was Uncle Hawk in World War I? That picture. I've never heard him mention it."

"No, as a matter of fact, he wasn't. He bought that uniform at an Army surplus store. He was running from the law then. I remember washing it for him, and Mama crying. We washed his clothes and sent them to him for over a year. Somebody would leave them off and pick them up."

"What was he in trouble for?"

"He escaped off a chain gang, for one thing. It was all because of drinking. You've heard it talked about. It was a real shame, but he's gone straight for a long time now. That other was a long time ago. Time changes some things."

I felt she wanted the topic closed.

I was about to bring up the question of Meredith and Mark going into service, and perhaps not being along next year, but I didn't. It didn't seem like the place or time. Yet, I wanted to explode with my concern so that this family would somehow register what was about to happen. They seemed to treat the imminent departure as a normal event. I wanted to shake them up, say, "Don't you all have something to *say* about this? Aren't you concerned?" They'll talk far more about Old Ross, Tyree, bird dogs, and cooking, than they will about these young men going away to war.

Day Two: Silver Springs. It was exciting again, and this was the first year Taylor got the full effect of all the wonderment. His favorite was the monkeys in the trees which we saw on the jungle cruise.

On the second night Aunt Sybil fixed quail casserole, one of her best dishes. Dan Braddock was there. The conversation got onto Vietnam. Meredith likes to call it B. F. Nam, because that's what Taylor calls it. At first I didn't want to get involved, but I got to thinking that I'd been a part of this family for ten years, a veritable decade.

"Nobody else in the family has gone to war, have they?" I asked.

"Thomas, Esther's husband," said Uncle Hawk.

"Blood kin, I mean."

Miss Esther eyed me. "Isaac, Walker's oldest, was killed in the Civil War. Ross's brother," she said.

"And Daddy was a frogman," said Noralee.

"And built bridges," said Mr. Copeland.

"But none of that counts," said Meredith, "because he never got any farther than Norfolk, Virginia."

"The timing's always been wrong," said Uncle Hawk, "since the Civil War, anyway. Like Thatcher there—he's got a kid and is too old."

Aunt Sybil passed the biscuits.

"Well, I'll just miss them being away for one thing," I said.

"Who was in the Civil War?" asked Dan Braddock.

"Isaac, Walker's boy, was killed, then Walker went in sometime, a couple of times, I think," said Uncle Hawk. "Turned around and came home the first time because they told him it was over. While he was gone Caroline threw boiling water on the Yankees. Did you ever hear about that, Frances?"

"Rhonda."

"I mean Rhonda. Excuse me, honey. It was Frances last year, wadn't it, Meredith?"

"You lie, Uncle Hawk."

"Anyway, Caroline threw boiling water on the Yankees."

"What did she do that for?" asked Rhonda.

"She was mad. They stole her meat and was sitting around in the front yard eating it."

"I'd been afraid they might have killed me if I'd done that."

"She won't afraid. Poured a pan of boiling water on them and said she wished they were dead and in the belly of hell. Next day Ross, who won't big as nothing, shot at them from out of a tree, a hollow tree, holed up in a hollow tree, and they couldn't find him. He climbed up the inside of a tree."

"Pass some of that casserole," said Dan Braddock. "Maybe Mark can fly that floatplane to Vietnam, Albert, and scare all the slant-eyes to death."

"It won't fly," said Meredith.

"That's what I mean," said Dan Braddock.

"I get me some bigger engines on it and it'll fly," said Mr. Copeland. "That's all it needs—a little more horsepower."

"You just need a horse," said Mildred, buttering a biscuit. "Or a mule. Keep figures on *him*." She looked up. "He's got a notebook with his figuring in it—on the floatplane. Plus all the children's heights and weights, and newspaper clippings and I don't know what all."

"I got two notebooks," said Mr. Copeland.

"Except the stuff on the floatplane ain't accurate," said Thatcher. Thatcher worries about that. I don't think it's all that important. The thing will fly or not fly regardless of what's in the notebooks. Except I guess the notebook would be a fun thing for Taylor to read once he's grown.

MARK

I remember being about ten, when Uncle Albert would sit in
his cloth beach chair in the front yard, holding his bird notebook that he'd drawn birds in—how they look when they're
flying. They weren't very good pictures.

He's quizzing Thatcher, Meredith, Noralee, and me. He
has his teeth out, so he's talking funny. A bird is flying over
the trees. "Whath that one, Noralee? Be quiet, Meredith."

"A crow."

"It's a buzzard!" says Meredith.

"I thaid be quiet. Give her another chance. Nexth time she
gets two chances. Everybody gets two chances from now on.
Underthand? Do you underthand, Meredith?"

"Yeth thir."

"Don't you mock me." He jumps, holding on to the chair
arms, like he's going to get up. Then he does this jaw motion,
where his chin goes up into his face. Then he sits back.

That night I'm staying at Meredith's.

Uncle Albert goes to bed early. Meredith begs Aunt Mildred to let us stay up and watch TV. She says okay.

The Channel 9 news signs off, and suddenly there is an F-104 Starfighter, climbing higher, then rolling into a lazy aileron roll.

"Look at that!" says Meredith.

The camera zooms in. A white-helmeted pilot is in the cockpit and there's this poem about slipping the surly bonds of earth and dancing the skies on laughter-silvered wings, and goes on to something about "reach out and touch the face of God."

"Man, that's something! Did you see that?"

"Yeah I saw it."

"Turn the station! Maybe it's on another station!"

"That's what I'm going to do," says Meredith. "I'm going to fly one of those."

"I am too."

"No, you're not. You can't go in the Air Force if your daddy got killed in the war. You can't go. It's going to be me."

I tell Mother I want to be a jet pilot, and she says, "If you were a doctor or a missionary you could fly to see your patients maybe, or whatever. But if you were just a pilot you wouldn't be able to be a doctor or a missionary—or a concert pianist."

BLISS

We were eating dessert when Dan Braddock said, "Mark, you're going to find you one of them slant-eyed girls to marry? They'll walk on your back and make you feel good."

"I don't know," said Mark. "I might end up staying in the States. That stuff might be over before too long. I'm not going to volunteer to go, but if I have to, I have to."

"Find you a slant-eye in the States then."

Rhonda looked at Meredith. "I'm going to check your back for footprints."

"Maybe he won't have to go over there either," I said.

"I wish," said Rhonda, "but that ain't what he told me."

"I'll probably go," said Meredith.

Then Thatcher got into his military arm talk, which pretty soon changed to talk about the next day's hunt. Mildred, Aunt Sybil, and Rhonda were talking about Silver Springs, and Miss Esther and Noralee were eating quietly. I wish Noralee would speak up more. She'll talk to me, but not much, unless we're alone.

I got to thinking that I would miss Meredith during the next three days of hunting, and Thatcher, but especially Meredith and Mark, in light of their going off in a few months. It occurred to me that I could go along on a hunting trip. Why not? I could join these men, be with them. For one day, at least—one of the three hunting days. But I dared not broach the subject in front of everybody at once.

I waited until later when the men had gone out to the guest house, just before we were settling in for the night, and I asked Rhonda, who had a rollaway bed in the living room, "Have you ever thought about going hunting with the men?"

"Nope. Shoot little birds? Fishing is hard enough for me."

"I think I might see about going one day."

"I don't think I'd like it."

That was enough for me. I went quietly out the back door so that I could knock on the guest house door, get Thatcher to come out, and ask him.

Meredith was sitting on the back steps, alone. It was cold.

I sat down beside him. "What are you doing out here?" I asked.

"Just thinking. Kind of." He looked at me and smiled. "And Rhonda's supposed to sneak out."

"Should I go back in?"

"Oh no. No."

So I sat. I had to say a few things. "You know, I think about you leaving a whole lot, Meredith. And nobody talks about it much, one way or the other. And coming down here makes it worse."

"Makes what worse?"

"Thinking about it. I don't know why. Because we're all together, I guess."

"It's just something I have to do, and then it'll be over."

He was wearing blue jeans worn thin at the knees—little fuzzies. I put my hand on his knee, the soft cloth, and rested my arm on his leg. "I wish you weren't going. That's all I can say."

The side of his face was lighted by the dull green light from the street light. "Hell, three years from tonight we'll be sitting right here," he said.

"I'll remember that," I said. We sat not moving. I could feel his leg and knee with my arm and hand. "You be sure to write me."

"I will."

"Good. Listen, what do you think about me going hunting with you-all tomorrow?"

"Why?"

"Just to see what it's like."

"Fine with me. Yeah. That'd be fun."

"I asked Rhonda. She didn't want to go."

"Yeah, it's all right with me. You might get a little tired, though."

I realized that I wanted to be Rhonda for a night. Just one night. But I knew the deep and sacred futility of such thinking.

"I guess I ought to ask Thatcher first," I said, standing.

"Tell Papa I'm watching some more TV."

I stood, walked to the guest room, and knocked. Mr. Copeland opened the door and stuck his head out. I got a glimpse of Mark in his underwear. "What ith it?" said Mr. Copeland.

"I want to ride along on the hunt tomorrow. Think that'll be okay?"

"You?"

"I just want to see what it's like."

"Okay. We'll make room. Damn, ith cold. Thee you in the morning. Thatcher'll come wake you up. We got the clock thet." He shut the door.

I knocked. The door opened.

"Meredith said to tell you he's watching TV," I said.

"He better get to bed."

I turned and started back to the house. The street light shone through the Spanish moss. Rhonda was sitting with Meredith on the back steps. The cold, damp air went straight through my clothes, through my skin, to my bones. Cold weather in Florida is very cold, because it's so damp, Florida being between two oceans, or an ocean and a gulf.

I walked up the steps past them.

"You going hunting tomorrow?" asked Rhonda.

"I'm not sure. I'm thinking about it. I think I'll see how cold it is. Good night, y'all."

The next morning at about five-thirty Thatcher came in and held my foot until I woke up. It was quite cold, even inside. Before we had gone to bed, Aunt Sybil put out a pair of her leather boots and extra socks since the boots were a little big. Thatcher had brought over some of Mr. Copeland's hunting clothes: pants equipped with extra thickness in front to guard against briars, hunting coat, flannel shirt, and black crewneck sweater. In the coat pocket was toilet paper and an apple. How practical! I rolled up the sleeves and pants legs.

We walked out the back door into the freezing damp darkness. There was a bright new moon. We walked across the yard and the road and into the back door of the store where Uncle Hawk was cooking breakfast. Mr. Copeland, Meredith, and Mark, dressed in their hunting clothes, sat around a small table in the kitchen.

Uncle Hawk was singing at the stove. I sat at the table with the others. I could tell that no one had strong objections to my going along. I happily anticipated being in on this ritual of the hunt, watching the dogs "work"—I'd heard so many exclamations about their exploits—and finally, spending some time with Meredith, and Mark, Thatcher.

"They ever tell you about Tyree and the hot coal?" Uncle Hawk asked me.

"No. I don't think so."

"He thought he saw a piece of chocolate on the floor one time—in front of the fireplace—picked it up and it burnt the hell out of him, but instead of hollering he handed it to his half-brother, Dink—said 'Here, Dink, you want some chocolate candy?' and Dink took it and it burnt the hell out of him, blistered him and left a scar, but it didn't burn Tyree at all—leastways it didn't leave any scar."

"I always thought that was Walker and one of his brothers," said Mr. Copeland.

"I know you did, but I told you I remembered it. I remember it happening. It must have been before you was born."

"Maybe so, but I always thought it was Walker."

We had a wonderful breakfast of bacon, eggs, toast, honey buns, maple syrup, and coffee—black. I didn't ask for cream since no one else was using it.

While we ate, Uncle Hawk and Mr. Copeland talked about

progress on the floatplane. We all thought that Mr. Copeland had given it up several years ago. But he hadn't. He's started back on it and last summer when Uncle Hawk was up for the gravecleaning, they towed it to Lake Blanca and drove it around on the water. Meredith says next time they go, he's going to get Rhonda's band, The Rockets, to come and set up on a flatbed truck and do the song she's writing about the floatplane.

It worries me because Mr. Copeland does the flying—or should I say, the floating—and he has had only a few flying lessons. He has a student license, I think, and claims that flying off water will be easier than flying off land because the whole big lake is your runway. Thank goodness, he will not let any of the children drive it. He say's he's the one built it and so he'll be the one to fly it—when he gets some bigger engines on it, and gets it balanced right. It worries Mildred to death.

After breakfast, Uncle Hawk sent Thatcher to the dog pen to get the dogs. I went along. They were so excited, jumping around in the pen, up on each other, vapor puffing from their mouths into the cold, damp air. Thatcher opened the door and they sprinted out, packed with energy and about to burst with excitement, running around, relieving themselves, then heading across the side road toward the jeep truck.

Bobby Simms, a little man who is Uncle Hawk's hunting partner, arrived in his jeep, three dogs in back; and we got all packed in and were off. I sat in Thatcher's lap for the drive, which started in darkness.

"How come you doing this?" asked Thatcher.

"I just want to see what you-all do."

"We shoot birds. We walk and shoot birds. You'll get tired."

"Maybe so."

The drive ended in the woods as the sun peeped through the trees. I was mortified to discover that we were hunting on posted land.

MARK

Uncle Hawk, fixing a great big breakfast in the cafe part of the store, sends Meredith into the grocery part to get honey buns for everybody. Uncle Albert goes with him. They pack up on cans of Vienna sausage and beans and boxes of crackers and cookies and stuff for the hunt. Bliss is going with us.

I can't wait. I mean I really look forward to this, and I went dove hunting enough this fall that I think I might be able to outshoot Meredith today.

Sometime before we start eating Uncle Hawk asks me, "You still got that little Fox Sterling?" I say yes.

Meredith and I were twelve: The guns were for sale at an estate auction, twenty gauge, double barrels. A Fox Sterling and a Remington. They were leaning against a wall between two rocking chairs on the front porch. A woman played a fiddle behind a microphone on the auctioneer's stand.

Uncle Albert picked up the guns and handed them to us. "How do they feel? That's a Fox, Mark. Good little gun."

"A fox?"

"A Fox Sterling. Good name. A good little gun."

The wood was worn smooth and not scratched. It dropped in line when I brought it to my shoulder, pointing out across a field. People saw me and I felt important.

"I won't be able to give more than forty dollars apiece," said Uncle Albert. "Somebody might outbid me."

The auctioneer auctioned chairs, swords, lamps, hall coatracks, sets of dinner plates.

It was time for the guns. The Fox was up first.

A man bid twenty-five dollars—before the auctioneer started. "I got a twenty-five. Five. Twenty-five. Who'll give me thirty? I got twenty-five. A fine shotgun. Who'll give me thirty?"

"Thirty," said Uncle Albert.

"I got thirty, thirty, thirty. Who'll give me thirty-five, thirty-five?"

The man raised his hand.

"I got thirty-five. Five. Thirty-five, five, five. Who'll give me forty? I got thirty-five."

Uncle Albert nodded.

I stared at the other man. He was wearing a loose brown shirt and green work pants. I wanted to run over and hold his arms down, pull him out of the crowd and away. He was standing very still. He had a cigarette in his hand. He brought his cigarette up to his mouth and took a deep draw, raised his hand with the cigarette between his fingers, and let the smoke out.

"I got forty-five, five. I got forty-five. Fifty?" The auctioneer looked at Uncle Albert, who was now, I knew, out of the race.

I remember thinking: the other man will walk up to the auctioneer, get the shotgun, walk out to his car, open the back door, slide the gun onto the back seat and close the door, get into the front seat, crank the car, and drive off down the road until he disappears, and I will never as long as I live see the gun again—the double-barreled Fox Sterling. The twenty-gauge, twenty-eight-inch barrel shotgun with the shining wood, well-oiled, smoothly clicking breach—the gun which will get me a place in the woods with Thatcher, Meredith, Albert, and the dogs, or with Meredith and the dogs, or walking alone way back in the woods, knowing where I am, able to head for home across broomstraw fields, up and down pinestraw covered banks, through thickets of honeysuckle and briars and poke weeds, and get back home tired, able to show Meredith whatever I killed.

"That gun is long gone," said Meredith.

I looked up at Uncle Albert. He looked down at me, and then back at the auctioneer. He nodded to the auctioneer.

"Fifty. I got fifty. Do I hear fifty-five?"

The man raised his hand.

My heart dropped.

Uncle Albert nodded.

"Sixty. I got sixty. Gimme sixty-five. Gimme sixty-five."

The man dropped his cigarette to the ground, twisted his foot on it, and shook his head.

"Sold. Sixty dollars. To this gentleman over here."

"Go get your gun, boy," said Uncle Albert.

Meredith got his for forty.

Uncle Hawk lowers the tailgate and the dogs jump up and scramble into the dog box. I slip my gun into the case Uncle Hawk gave me. It has a worn felt lining. Meredith climbs up into the cab. I follow and sit at the window. Uncle Albert, Thatcher, and Bliss are riding with Bobby Simms. I think Bliss wanted to ride with Meredith.

About ten minutes or so beyond Burgaw we turn onto a dirt road. After about a mile, Uncle Hawk slows down to almost a stop and drives the truck across a shallow ditch and into the open woods. He stops the truck near a barbed-wire fence about twenty feet from the road, gets out, cuts a small pine branch with his hunting knife, goes back and erases the tire tracks across the ditch. With a screwdriver and hammer he separates the barbed-wire strands from a couple of posts on either side of one standing loose in the ground. With Meredith helping, he pulls the loose post up out of the ground —with the wire still attached—and forces it to lie flat. Then he drives the truck across the wire. Bobby Simms follows. This is what we do every year, and I know Bliss can't believe it. The women weren't supposed to know. Uncle Hawk sticks the pole back into its hole, then we ride on into the woods and stop. The dogs are bumping around in the dog house.

We make plans to meet at the canal crossing for lunch. Bobby Simms drives off, leaving me, Meredith, and Uncle Hawk together. Bliss says she wants to hunt with us, but Thatcher says we can switch around at lunch.

When they are almost out of sight, Uncle Hawk opens the doghouse door. The dogs scramble out, run, stop, sniff, pee, then run again with their noses to the ground.

"Call it, Meredith," says Uncle Hawk. He flips a coin.

"Heads."

"It's tails. You get to ride the tractor seat, Mark."

I climb up onto the hood and then sit in the seat with my feet on the big wooden front bumper. It's my job to watch for stumps and holes, and watch the dogs for a point.

"If we run up a covey, pop you one," says Uncle Hawk. The truck starts forward. The seat moves beneath me like an elephant head, bumping and rolling slowly, moving along through the woods in Africa. I check my gun safety switch —it's on—and lay the gun across my lap, thumb on the safety, index finger resting against the trigger guard.

We hit a hole, come up out of it. Meredith sticks his head out the window and says to me, "Get your head out your ass."

I suddenly see Joe, my dog, standing on the rim of a rise in some tall pines, pointing. Old Joe. Nick is about thirty yards behind him, backing—between us and Joe. Uncle Hawk sees them and stops the truck. I crawl down quietly. Uncle Hawk and Meredith get out of the truck. No one speaks. I check my thumb on the safety switch. We spread out, and side by side, start walking up the rise toward Joe. I look at Meredith. He looks at me and makes a face with his eyes great big. This is it. When we are near Nick, Uncle Hawk talks softly. "Easy, boy. Easy, boy." We walk past him. Nick follows us—still on a point, moving only his legs, carefully, silently. Uncle Hawk looks around for the other dogs. I see Banjo, Uncle Hawk's best dog, far beyond the truck, hunting. I look back at Joe up ahead, pointed. I wonder if the fur is raised along his rump. That's Joe's sign: rump-fur raised—birds for sure. Nick's sign is raised fur on his neck. I don't know about Banjo.

I look at Joe's rump. He is too far away to tell. Uncle Hawk,

turning his head, says, "Easy, Nick." Nick follows silently.
The hair *is* raised along Joe's rump, stiff as a hair brush.
He is standing still, his tail high in the air, looking straight
ahead, his rear to us. My heart is thumping against my ribs,
up in my neck and ears. Old Joe is doing great. My feet make
soft brushing sounds in the weeds. My eyes are watering. The
hairline above my eyes prickles. I blink tears. I check my
thumb on the safety.

We are getting close to Joe. "Easy, boy," Uncle Hawk says.
"Keep walking, boys."

We walk very slowly. A step, then another step. I look at the
white fur raised stiff on Joe's rump. Joe is exactly between
Meredith and me, frozen still. In a line are Uncle Hawk, Meredith, Joe, me. I blink tears, look for birds on the ground
ahead. The birds have to be just ahead, there in a thick cover
of lespedeza, white with frost. Joe remains motionless. We
walk past him.

"They're right here, boys," says Uncle Hawk.

My heart pounds. The birds are about to explode up in
front of our faces. I know it. There is no sign of anything
there on the ground in front of me except the frost-covered
lespedeza. The birds are hidden, and still. I can hardly get
my breath.

The ground suddenly rises: quail, thundering up and away.
I bring the gun to my shoulder, watching a single bird among
all the others, as if he's painted there on the backdrop of
trees to stay forever until I get the gun on him and pull the
trigger. I am pulling the trigger. Pulling. Then squeezing.
The gun will not fire. The trigger is hung. I squeeze, pull,
squeeze again. The other two shotguns blast away.

The birds are gone. Uncle Hawk is moving out ahead, talking to Joe. "Dead bird. Dead bird, Joe."

My safety is still on. I forgot to click the safety switch forward. Shit, shit, shit.

"Did you get one?" Meredith asks me.

"Don't think so. You?"

"I got one. Straight ahead. Uncle Hawk, did you shoot that one straight ahead?"

"Both mine came left. He's yours."

"I think I hit one, but he kept going," I say.

"I know I got one," says Meredith. "One–nothing. Ha."

Uncle Hawk calls the dogs in and they find the three dead birds and we start back to the jeep.

"You boys hear about Tyree on Rob Tucker's land that was posted?" says Uncle Hawk.

"No."

We always say no whether we have or not.

"Tyree shoots a bird and old man Tucker comes over and says 'Tyree, where'd you shoot that bird?' and Tyree says, 'I shot him in the ass, I reckon, Rob—he was flying *from* me.'" Uncle Hawk laughs. "Old Mr. Tucker was 'the sort who painted his hair and was a mite high-strung.' That's what Tyree said about him."

At noon we stop at the canal crossing for lunch. I am very hungry. It has warmed up a good bit, but it's still cold.

Uncle Hawk spreads newspapers—for a tablecloth—across the truck hood and gets out the food: cans of Vienna sausage, pork and beans, sardines, loafbread, crackers, cookies, apples, oranges, and coffee. He opens a sack and gets out paper plates and plastic spoons.

On the side of the truck, in front of the rear wheel well, is a water tank with a spigot. I hold a tin pan under the spigot. The water sounds in the pan. The dogs crowd in, tongues lapping. I push the pan toward Joe. His throat rests on the upturned underside of my wrist. I feel his throat muscles and his loose, furry skin move on my wrist.

I hear Bobby Simms's jeep coming.

They've had good luck. Bliss is smiling. She asks Meredith how many birds he's shot. Meredith tells her that he got eight and that I got four.

"I shot four of his and didn't tell him," I say.

We all crowd around the hood of Uncle Hawk's jeep and eat. The dogs know to stay back. Uncle Hawk throws them slices of bread.

"You boys going to make it down next year?" asks Bobby Simms, with a cracker in his mouth, spooning sardines onto his plate. Bobby Simms is short, older than Uncle Hawk, and chain-smokes Luckies.

"I don't know. I'm supposed to be in pilot training."

"You know what kind of airplane you'll be flying?"

I'm so glad he asked I don't know what to do. "T-37's and T-38's mostly. T-37 for about four months and the T-38 for about six months. The T-37's kinda small. The T-38 looks like a white Coke bottle, shaped kind of like that." I see it in my mind; I see and feel myself in it. "It's supersonic. The first supersonic trainer."

"How about you, Bud?" he says to Meredith.

I'm thinking, *Supersonic, man. Doesn't that register?*

"I'll be in the Marines," says Meredith. "I'll be doing all the work while he's flying around in the sky, counting trees and talking on his radio."

"I wish they didn't have to go," says Bliss. Her coat is too big and she's got on one of Uncle Hawk's hunting caps with the earflaps down—too big. She's eating beans from a paper plate. "Somebody's got to go," says Bobby Simms, his mouth full. Then he talks about people burning their draft cards, saying they all ought to be set on fire themselves. Thatcher says every country has to have a military arm, and I say the civilian leaders decide whether or not to have a military arm and then the military arm has to do all it can to win any war the civilian leaders believe has to be fought. But I'm thinking that Vietnam might be over in a year. Then I can fly all training missions for five years while I'm deciding whether to stay in or get out and do something with my degree—Industrial Relations. But if I'm one of the ones who has to go to Vietnam, that's the decision I made when I decided to be part of the military arm.

I can see me sitting in a cockpit wearing a white helmet.

We finish lunch and load up the dogs. Uncle Albert and I go with Bobby Simms. Meredith, Thatcher, and Bliss go with Uncle Hawk.

That afternoon we find four or five coveys and I miss far more than I hit.

When it's almost dark, Sam points a single in a patch of palmetto. "Okay, you're due," Uncle Albert says to me, almost whispering. "Get on up there and pop him. We'll stay back here. Walk right on past Nick and kick in those palmettos. Shoot him in the ass if he's flying straight away. But he'll probably turn left toward that cover. Let the gun move through him, right on in front of him, and shoot with the gun still moving. Like I showed you."

"Yessir."

I walk up behind Nick, holding my gun ready to bring to my shoulder, then beside Nick. I kick the palmetto, my eyes watering, heart pounding. Nick suddenly pounces, then freezes again. One, then another bird explodes up. They are going away fast. They fly straight away, then turn left as I click the safety, let the barrel catch up, swing through them, and in front of them, squeezing the trigger for the blast in my face as the second quail tumbles to the ground and bounces once.

"Good shot!" says Uncle Albert.

"Dead bird, Joe," I say. The other dogs come running. Joe sees the bird, pounces on it, picks it up in his mouth and retrieves. It's a hen. She holds her head up, looking around, so I grab the head and hold tight and twist until the neck pops. Her body quivers. I wait. Get it over with, I think. Hurry. The quivering continues in my hand, vibrates through my hand, arm, shoulder, chest. I want her to hurry and die, to get this over with. I twist the head again. The quivering begins to slow. I stick her, still quivering lightly, into the game pouch of my hunting coat.

I figure I haven't been leading them enough. That's it. I've been shooting behind them, and if they are flying straight away, too soon. I've got it figured out, but it is late in the day and we are through hunting.

BLISS

The hunt was exhausting, and I got to shoot a gun. Meredith, Thatcher, Bobby Simms, and I were at the meeting place, standing around after hunting all day, when Meredith says, "Don't you want to shoot my gun?"

"No. Doesn't it hurt your shoulder?"

"Not if you squat down and lean back on your heels. Look, here's all you do." He squatted, leaned back, brought his gun to his shoulder. "Boom. Nothing to it. I'll put a tin can on that stump. You can shoot it."

"I don't think so."

"Look, if you come hunting you've got to shoot a shotgun, at least once."

"You promise it won't hurt my shoulder?"

"I promise. You just hold it real loose. Here, come over here."

"Thatcher, will it hurt?"

"Oh no. Not if you squat like that. Aim down the barrel at the tin can."

I don't know why I didn't see it coming. I did everything just like Meredith said. Thatcher, Meredith, and Bobby Simms stood back. I squatted, leaned back on my heels and when I pulled the trigger there was a terrible kick to my shoulder and I of course toppled right back onto my behind. They all laughed.

It was an interesting experience all in all, and I'm glad I went, but it takes more stomach than I've got to shoot birds over and over all day long, some of the birds being only wounded when they fall. And sometimes one will be shot down and can run, but not fly, and it won't be found.

On returning, I cleaned only one bird, then Mildred and I went in the house. I took a wonderful hot bath and went to bed early. Tired as I was, I couldn't go to sleep for a long time.

MARK

When we get back, Meredith and I put up the dogs. They are
tired. I pour the stale water out of the pail which sits just
inside the pen gate, rinse away the little bit of fungus, then
fill the pail with fresh, cold water. I pat Joe on the shoulder
and talk to him a little bit. He did great.

Meredith says, "Next time we're here at the same time
might be five or six years from now. We'll be married and
have kids."

"Naw, we can get leave and come down here together and
hunt. If I can get stationed at Homestead, or McGill, it'll be
close. And you might be down this way. Somewhere close
—for a while anyway."

"What if this was the last time we hunted down here. Hell,
we might be dead next year this time."

"That's crazy, Meredith. The chances are very slim. Very
slim."

"I think about it."

Uncle Hawk comes with dog food in a bucket and portions it out into seven dog pans. The dogs stand back. Prancing in place, saliva stringing from their mouths, they look at Uncle Hawk. He stands for a few seconds, then suddenly shouts, "Eat!"

They jump to it, eating in big gulps.

Meredith and I stay and watch them for a few minutes, then we walk to the table under the shed behind the store. Uncle Hawk has already dumped birds out on the table and started cleaning them. He picks up a bobwhite, pulls feathers from the wings and tail, pulls off the head, and then tears a little hole in the breast skin and skins it, as if ripping off a sweater right down to the feet. Then he breaks off the legs. He picks the feather stubs left at the wings and tail, knifes smoothly upward between the breast and backbone, reaches up and in with two fingers, pulls out the guts and the tiny brown-purple heart and liver, and flings the insides down into a paper sack. He scrapes inside the bird with the knife, dips the headless and naked thing down into—and back up out of—a big pan of reddish water, scrapes it inside again with the knife, then turns it loose into the water where it sinks, wing stubs outstretched, to the bottom of the pan, underwater with the others.

"Simple as pie," says Uncle Hawk to Bliss.

I pick up a bird, another bobwhite, and hand it to Bliss. She looks at it, turns it around. I pick up another. Its head is turned to one side, stiff, matted. I hold the little hard knob and pull. It holds. I pull harder and it begins to string loose, then separates from the body. I drop the head, a fuzzy marble, into the paper sack.

"Here," says Meredith to Bliss. He takes her bird. "Let me show you. Like this. Just stretch the wing out and you can grab the feathers and pull them out. See?"

I straighten a wing. The feathers fan out, overlapping, creating a design. They are hard to pull out—not like the tail feathers, which pop out softly.

"Now tear open the skin at the breast," Meredith says to Bliss.

"What's that soft spot in there?" she asks.

"That's the craw. Now look here, you can pull that right on out. Look a there. Peas. Now just skin him."

"Just skin him?"

"Just skin him."

I'm skinning mine. I tear a tiny hole at the breast and the skin and feathers pull away easily—down to the legs. I break away the legs. They snap like wet wooden matches. I run a finger across the bare flesh. It is cool, dry, smooth.

On the trip back to North Carolina, Rhonda keeps calling Bliss "the great white hunter." Part of the time Rhonda sits between Meredith and me in the back seat. Sometimes her leg is pretty tight against mine, and I remember standing beside her in the bar at the Club Oasis, and I wonder if she ever told Meredith about us going skinny-dipping or the time way before that when she unbuttoned her blouse in the barn with those little kittens crawling all over her.

One summer, a long time ago, Rhonda's family moved into the house out across the field behind my house, the field full of green vegetables that Uncle Albert was raising—low-growing vegetables like peas and snapbeans, no corn that year. You could see straight across the field. I would look across the field through the clear, wavering heat dancing up from the green vegetables. At one time, for a while, I had played over in her yard with her brother, Terry, but had to stop after Mother brought me out in our backyard one day to hear Mr. Gibbs's loud, drunk voice, floating over to us, over the yellow butterflies darting above the vegetables.

Then Mother, standing in the kitchen, turning chicken in flour—talked to me about Mr. Gibbs. "He's an evil man, Mark —that Randall Gibbs. Coming home all hours, drunk. It's the work of the Devil. I don't want you over there around it. You understand?"

I saw the Gibbs house—full of all the Gibbs—sinking into the ground and going on down and down, finally landing in the firelakes of hell where it burned, with all the Gibbs in it, flames licking through and around it, for eternity.

"Mark, do you understand?"

"Yes ma'am."

She wrapped me in her arms—her white, floured hands not touching me—and prayed out loud that I would all my life shun the temptation of drink.

And then the skinny-dipping—the summer before I started at East Carolina, four years ago. Meredith had dropped out of Listre Community College and started to work as a lineman.

One night I park at the Club Oasis, in the dirt parking lot full of big, washed-out holes. I'm driving the Ford, which is dressed in a chrome tailpipe extension and the hubcaps that Meredith and I worked on in the shop.

Over the side entrance to the old brick school building is an unlit, broken neon sign: CLUB OASI.

I walk through the open doorway. There is a table and chair just inside the door, but no one is there. The hall has a wooden floor, and gives off echoes of my footsteps. The class-rooms are all closed except the last one, the bar. I look in: red lights. Someone is moving boxes. I walk straight ahead through swinging saloon doors into the auditorium. The seats have been removed and there are little holes in the floor where screws once held down rows of seats. There is a stage, without a curtain, and a row of empty sockets for footlights.

A member of the band, The Sierras, is setting up equipment.

"I guess I'm the piano player," I say. "I'm supposed to sit in for Rodney."

"Great. I'm John. You're Mark?"

"Right."

"You work with the tapes?"

"Oh yeah. I think I got everything worked out."

"Great. Listen, would you go back out to that car beside the door—blue Chevy—and get that amplifier in the back seat? I'll get us a beer. They're free for the band."

My mouth opens. I am saying no thank you. Mother is saying no thank you. I'm five or six, lying on a blanket in the yard with Mother on a moonless night when the sky is clear and the stars are thick, and she talks about God and the heav-ens and the millions and millions of stars, and how it will be wonderful when I'm old enough to learn to play the piano. She will buy a piano and I can learn to play from Mrs. Thomp-son and I will always be glad I learned because I can play hymns at church, and at other times when people are together and need a piano player. And I may grow up to be a concert pianist and dedicate my body and mind and soul to Christ.

Clean living and performing for the glory of God. And I visualize the white and black keys of a piano, my hands on the keys, moving, making the sounds, the clear sounds of a song. My Sunday school teachers—Mr. Tillman, Mr. Stokes, Mr. Umstead—are saying no, no thank you, no beer, no alcohol. My Sunday school students—Kenny Clere, Tom Dunn, Phil Register—aunts, the Bible, Jesus, Paul, Peter, Doubting Thomas, and God are all saying no thank you. But there is no sound. Only the noise of a box sliding across the floor in the bar.

I start to speak again. Then I figure I will just let the beer sit there. No need to say anything. I turn and walk out of the auditorium, down the hall, staring straight ahead—through the far open door at the clear, yellow horizon.

I come back with the amplifier. Two cold, sweaty, heavy cans of Budweiser beer are on the edge of the stage.

"We're really glad you could make it," said John. "Piano players are hard to come by, 'less it's some girl or something." He walks to the edge of the stage, stands beside the cans of beer. I am standing down on the auditorium floor. He sits down on the stage, picks up his beer and takes a swallow. "I didn't ask what you wanted. Hope a Bud is okay."

"Yeah. Fine."

I look around at all the space in the open auditorium, the empty corners, floor. Just a swallow, I think; I can just try it. I won't have to drink it all. I can just taste. It won't hurt me just to taste it. It certainly won't make me sick. I can leave the rest of it sitting here. Just a taste. I look around the auditorium again, pick up the can quickly, put it to my lips, turn it up, back down. The taste is metallic, carbonated, cold, strong.

Not so bad. Not so bad. It is all right. It is okay to taste it.

"That'll help you tickle them ivories," says John.

At ten forty-five we stop for our second break. I've finished four beers. The very top of my head is somehow dizzy, my eyes feel strained in a comfortable way, and my cheeks are beginning to numb. I watch the people on the dance floor move toward the bar. I know Meredith isn't coming tonight. He, Thatcher, and Uncle Albert are at the races in Franklinton. I scan for Rhonda but don't see her. I think about the time she unbuttoned her blouse. I walk to the steps at the edge of the stage, stop and look again, walk down the steps, onto the dance floor and into the bar.

Suddenly a hand is resting just above my left hip, one finger through a belt loop. I turn my head, look into Rhonda's eyes, speak from a dream: "Well, well, howdy. Good afternoon."

"Howdy. I, I didn't think we was ever going to get here. I come with Snodie Smith. Did Meredith go to the races?"

"Oh, yeah."

We fill an empty space at the counter.

"I might need a ride home," she said. "I don't know yet. If I do, can I ride with you?"

"Sure. Sure. That'll be fine. Just dandy."

"I'm going to sing in a band myself," she says. "I've already started. We been practicing. We already got a piano player, though. I wish we didn't. Danny Driscoll. You know him?"

"Yeah, I know Danny."

We stand at the bar. Her finger rests in my belt loop. "Have you all played 'I Need Your Loving Every Day'?" she asks.

"Not yet, but we're 'pose to."

"I love that song to death."

"I'll personally see iss de'cated you."

"You will?"

"Sure will. Now what did you say your name is?"

We laugh, heads falling back, as Rhonda presses—from hip to knee—against me. I take a deep swallow of beer, and Rhonda, bright-eyed, blond, red-lipped, holding the rim of her beer can against her teeth, looks at me with what I believe is, and fear is, and know is—and far away inside pray isn't —lust and hope.

After the last song, the band members tell me I've done a great job. I thank them. It was wonderful. I want to do it again. I tell them I'd love to play again—anytime. I look around for Rhonda but don't see her. I am very dizzy. Then I see her come through the swinging saloon doors with a beer in her hand. She looks up at me, walks up the stage stairs, over to me and grabs my shirt at the elbow. "Snodie Smith said you are as good as Jerry Lee Lewis."

"Well. Well, well."

As best as I can, I help the boys pack up the band equipment. Rhonda helps.

We walk to the Ford. It's a hot night.

"God," says Rhonda, "I could use a swim. Where'd you get them hubcaps?"

"Bought them." I don't tell her they're the ones that came with the car, and Meredith and I sanded the black paint from every other little pie-slice section and painted them white.

"They're snazzy."

I open her door.

About a mile down the road, Rhonda slips over against me. "Do you mind if I sit a little closer?" she says.

"I don' mind."

She leans over into the back seat. "God, it's hot," she says, and as she rolls down the window behind me, her breast moves steadily, warmly, heavily against my shoulder. "I wouldn't mind taking a little swim," she said. "How about you?"

"I don' mind."

We do. I stand on the pond bank in my shorts while Rhonda, naked, side-strokes through the water lit by the moon, silent ripples spreading out from her body. I glimpse a dark nipple and then Lord, oh Lord, she gets out and walks up close enough for me to see—in the moonlight—goose pimples on her breasts around those tight-standing nipples and I lose my breath thinking about Brigitte Bardot and birth and death. She leans against me cool and wet and my heart pounds and pounds as I feel nausea and dizziness and then I mumble and chicken my way out of everything but the drive home. Rhonda drives.

At breakfast next morning, I say only a few words.

"Do you feel all right?" Mother asks.

"Yes ma'am."

I always drive to Sunday school, let Mother off in front of the church, and then park the car in the parking lot.

I stop the car in front of the church. Mrs. Bingham is standing there. Mother says hello to Mrs. Bingham through her open window, then opens the door, places her right foot on the ground, and sits there talking. I glance in the floorboard and see, looped around her black high heel: a white bra strap. The shoe on Mother's foot is slowly dragging the whole bra out from under the seat as she talks to Mrs. Bingham.

I dive for the shoe, lift it, unloop the bra strap from around the heel, grab the bra, press it against the floor while wadding it into a tiny ball, pull it to my chest, pause, stick it beneath me on the seat. I'll put it in the trash can in the bathroom in the church.

"What are you doing, Mark?!"

"Just getting some of this junk out of the floorboard."

"What junk? Mark, you've been acting mighty funny this morning."

"Just some old rags."

"Why are you sitting on them?"

"I just am. Get out. How are you today, Mrs. Bingham?"

"Fine," says Mrs. Bingham. "You?"

"Fine."

Mother looks at Mrs. Bingham, at me, then starts getting out, slowly.

As soon as she closes the door I speed off. I look in the rearview mirror. Mrs. Bingham is talking to Mother, who is staring at the back of the car.

1968

BLISS

Everybody carried on at the gravecleaning today as if nothing at all were irregular, even though Meredith and Mark are all but packed to leave. There weren't quite as many people as usual, but Uncle Hawk and Aunt Sybil and Dan Braddock did drive up from Florida, and Aunt Scrap was there, of course. And since it was my eleventh gravecleaning, it was also the eve of my tenth wedding anniversary. It's hard to believe.

I almost decided to bake a going-away cake for Meredith and Mark, but nothing I might write on the cake worked at all, so I brought my normal lemonade and brownies.

Mark's home dog, Trader, died in the winter, and he and Meredith took him down to the old Hope Road sawmill, that's abandoned, and buried him. It's where the family has buried all their dead dogs and I suppose if they erected tombstones down there, it would look like Arlington.

Meredith's home dog, Fox, is still alive, but Mr. Copeland has been saying he needs to be put to sleep.

Fox and Trader always got along fine with Aunt Sybil's little dog, Dixie B., but Mark's new dog, Rex, went crazy barking when Aunt Sybil got out of the Cadillac at the graveyard holding Dixie B. in her arms. So Fox started in barking too, and Aunt Sybil had to get back in the car and take Dixie B. back to the Copeland's and lock her on the back porch. It was embarrassing to me. Sometimes I don't know about all these dogs.

Rhonda was not there at first. She came at lunchtime. She and Meredith have decided not to get married right away and I think that's a good idea. They've had fusses and fights off and on lately—Meredith wants her to stop singing in the rock and roll band.

Then sometime after the Christmas trip to Florida, Mark confessed to Meredith about going skinny-dipping with Rhonda several years ago. Meredith told me.

It would be very, very unfair—and reckless—if Rhonda has played these boys off against each other in some secretive manner. I don't think Rhonda has realized that she's playing with dynamite.

THE VINE

Walker's brother Julius who lived across the road died after a fist fight with Walker before they had occasion to make up. The fight was about a debt and while Walker had Julius down in the road between their houses Julius bit Walker's finger and it was always crooked afterward.

Julius and Walker didn't speak to each other for two days. Then Julius became sick with influenza and was inside for a week. Walker was on the way over there with a chess pie made by Caroline when he met Julius's wife Rebecca in the road coming over to tell them that Julius had died. A doctor from Raleigh arrived too late.

Caroline came out at bedtime and sat beside Walker on the steps. It's time for bed Walker.

I don't think I'll be able to sleep tonight.

You should get your rest.

He might as well been a Yankee as far as our feelings.

T'warn't nothing. You both would have been over it in no time.

I'd liked to have asked him what I might do for his place. The ceremony at the graveyard was larger than any of the others. Rebecca had so much food she brought the overflow from their house.

On the next blue moon, Thomas, Bertha, and Julius appeared in their rockers.

"Do these children cry like that all the time?" asked Julius.

"Yes," said Bertha. "Give them a little push in the cradle. . . . that helps. I'm afraid that last one down there was born dead like my grandson. We never hear it at all. Can you see in there?"

"Well." Julius stretched his neck. "Well, I don't know if it's dead or not, but it's got a foot bigger'n mine."

MARK

It's the last gravecleaning before I leave for El Paso, and Meredith for Parris Island.

I finish raking pine straw, get the ax from the truck bed, stop by where Aunt Scrap is sitting and talk to her for a few minutes, then call Rex and start over to the wisteria to cut it with an ax from around all the trees I can get to. All of them maybe. The wisteria is going to kill them. It wraps around and chokes them. The stuff has gone completely wild.

Uncle Hawk says it won't make any difference, that I can't kill it with an ax. Meredith calls me to walk down to the rock pile, so I put the ax back in the truck and go with him.

We walk through the pines. "Why you going down there?" I ask.

"The rocks around Tyree's grave. There's about four little ones where it needs two big ones."

I need to say something about us leaving. "You think there's any chance of you staying in?"

"Naw. Two years will be plenty. See some action. You're the one'll stay in. Get to sleep in a bed, make big money."

I don't know if he's jealous or what. It's not my fault he didn't go to college. "It won't be bad. I'll be glad to get the hell out of here."

"Don't forget to go to church."

"Yeah."

Thirty yards ahead, down the hill, I see the rock pile—a mound under pine straw. When this was a field, big white rocks were piled up so that plowing would be easier. One of Uncle Hawk's earliest memories is seeing Old Ross counting silver money on a table, money he'd gotten from under the rock pile to take to town and put in a bank.

"Y'all decided when you're going to get married?" I say. "If you could get to Vietnam and get that over, then Rhonda could meet you—in Hawaii. Y'all could get married in Hawaii or somewhere."

"Listen, Mark." Meredith stopped walking. I stopped. The rock pile was about ten feet ahead. "Why the hell did you have to tell me that about you and Rhonda?"

"What?"

"Skinny-dipping. I mean, why did you have to tell me? You could have kept shut up about it."

"I don't know. I just felt like I ought to tell you."

"Well, shit, why should I want to hear that?"

"I don't know. I didn't think it would make any difference."

"It makes one hell of a lot of difference. Wouldn't it to you?"

"I don't know."

"She never took *me* skinny-dipping. What if I'd gone skinny-dipping with some girl you were dating?"

"Shit, Meredith, she's going to marry *you.*"

"Yeah, but you did that right under my nose."

"That was a long time ago, Meredith, and she suggested it, I mean, she, I mean, it wasn't just all me, you know. It was us. Hell, I was drunk. It was just some fun."

"That's exactly what I know: it was just some fun; she suggested it. How the hell do I know what else she's done?"

"I don't guess you do, but she hasn't done anything with me, and she wants to marry you, Meredith. Why can't you just forget it?"

"You can't just decide to forget some things."

"I'm sorry. I'm really sorry. I hope something as little as that don't keep you-all from getting married."

"You thought it was funny."

"I didn't think it was funny—in any way that matters. Hell, Meredith, you used to think it was funny. You'd talk about getting Rhonda hot when we went frog gigging and stuff."

"Shit, Mark you don't. . . You need a daddy, or somebody, to teach you about women."

He turns and walks to the rock pile and starts pushing back pine straw and mulch. He rolls out a big white rock, then another. I'm trying to think of something to say. "If there's some way to forget it, that's what I'd like to do," I say.

"Sure."

He picks up one of the big, heavy rocks. "Get that other one. Let's go."

I bend down, pick up the rock in both hands.

BLISS

Quilts and lawn chairs were spread in their customary fashion around Mr. Copeland's truck so that we could eat our customary picnic. Rhonda, looking quite ravishingly striking, joined us before Meredith and Mark came back from the rock pile. She walked into the woods a little way to meet them as they trudged up carrying two large rocks to place in a ring of rocks around one of the graves.

Once we all got started on the sumptuous food, Meredith said, "I'm going to be buried right over there. I want to make it official."

"This graveyard is full," said Aunt Scrap. "That was decided a long time ago."

"Why?"

"Well, I don't know exactly. It just feels right. For one thing, it's way down here in the woods, and one of these days it's going to be all growed over with that wisteria vine. I got me a plot at the church. You do too, don't you, Esther?"

"Oh, yes. A big one, for Mark and his family and all."

"They never shipped home Thomas, did they?" asked Dan Braddock.

"No," said Miss Esther, looking at Mr. Braddock, "they didn't."

"Let's talk about something else," I said.

"I know Hawk and Sybil got a plot in Florida," said Mr. Copeland, "and we got that one out at Oak Hill."

"It's pretty out there," said Aunt Scrap.

"Well, I always wanted to be on that rise looking out across that pretty scenery to them far hills. This place just always seemed like a place to clean off. But I don't care; if you want to be buried here, it's fine with me," he said, looking at Meredith.

"It ought to stay like it is," said Aunt Scrap.

Meredith walked over to a clear spot, and marked an X with the heel of his shoe. "X marks the spot."

Every time I thought about Meredith being away in the Marines, a piece of biscuit would get hung in my throat, seem very large, and make my throat ache and my eyes water. And I knew Miss Esther had to be beside herself—her only son leaving, her husband having left for World War II, never to return. I wondered if he had come to the gravecleanings.

"Hand me one of them ham-and-biscuits," said Thatcher. "Whose are these?"

"Mine," said Aunt Scrap.

"That's good ham."

"I dipped it in red-eye gravy."

"There's your damn red-eye," said Uncle Hawk.

"What's that?" said Aunt Scrap.

"I said, 'There's your damn red-eye!'"

"Oh yeah—Ross and the striking iron."

I realized I was about to be subjected to yet another family story. Sometimes. . . .

"We all heard that one," said Aunt Scrap. "What do you young'uns know about Aunt Vera?" she said to Meredith and Rhonda.

"She used to drink bitters," said Meredith, "and she got a Civil War pension and—"

"Confederate pension."

"And her chickens roosted on her bed and she had a black dog named Sailor and she lived right down there." Meredith pointed.

"You do know something. You know what she used to say to that dog?"

"I don't know that. I won't here then."

"She'd tell him to get out the door, and he'd go under her table. So she'd say, 'Well, git under the table then.'"

"Tell about how she smelt," said Mr. Copeland.

"No need to talk about that," said Miss Esther.

"Well, it's a fact," said Aunt Scrap. She spat a stream of tobacco juice—sort of over Uncle Hawk's shoulder.

"Watch it," Uncle Hawk said, ducking. "Don't you spit on me."

"You be quiet. You just want to tell about Ross and the red-eye. Oh, I forgot. The bitters—she'd make a concoction and drink it for medicine. Did you just say that?" she asked Meredith.

"Yes ma'am, I did."

"What was in it?" asked Noralee.

"Seems like, oh, lion's tongue and cherry bark. I think that's right. But it's a fact about her smell. I slept with her more than once, and I guess we didn't pay it no mind, but I don't think she ever washed anything but her feet, and that dog Sailor.slept on the foot of the bed, and Lord knows, chickens would come in there and roost on her bed, and lay eggs on it. That ain't no lie. It was a feather bed and the feathers, even when it was mashed down, was as thick as that." She held her hands apart. "And bless her heart, that there baby, that BORN DED, was hers."

THATCHER

Meredith and Mark will be leaving for military service in a week or two. It's unfortunate, but there is no denying the fact that the rest of the world is not as civilized as the United States, and democracy has its price. Sometimes a high price. Of course, this Vietnam thing might be over before they get there. I hope so.

Anyway, Saturday when we left the graveyard, we left the truck—loaded with all the tools—for Meredith and Rhonda so they could load in the lawn mower when they finished. Meredith wanted to stay and mow the lawn. Aunt Scrap won't let him do it when we're all down there because it makes too much noise to talk over. The women went somewhere, and Papa, Uncle Hawk, Mr. Braddock, Mark, and me walked to the shop so Uncle Hawk could see what Papa has done on the floatplane since last year.

I swear. Papa and the floatplane.

Uncle Hawk was thumbing through the notebooks. He got

to the very last entry which had such and such a date and then it said: "Dropped engine."

"What's that, Albert?" says Uncle Hawk. "You just going to use one engine now?"

"No. Why?"

"It says here 'dropped engine.'"

"Oh no. It dropped—*fell*—fell on the floor."

"Fell on the floor?"

"Just a little bump."

"Sure," I said.

What happened was, he had two chain block-and-tackles, which I got wholesale through Strong Pull, hanging from two rafters in the ceiling, each one holding a motor, because Papa pulls the motors up, see, then sets them down and bolts them to different places on the fuselage looking for what he calls better balance. He uses two rafters so there's not too much weight on one, and then he moves the plane from one place to another while he's working on it. It's pretty light. And so one of the engines ended up hanging from a rafter out over a wing. All we could figure out later was that that rafter was weak from where a knot was in the wood—it was weak all along and we didn't know it.

I was out there in the shop, sharpening my knives, when I heard a little crack in the rafter. Papa took a step toward the plane, the rafter popped loud, the engine fell, hit on top of the wing, knocked that wing down, the other wing up, catching him right in the chin and knocking him back against the tool cabinet.

Mama thought maybe that was the end of the floatplane, but Papa started in ordering fresh aluminum tubing. ⌐

So, anyway, we're waiting for Meredith and Rhonda to bring the truck so we can hook up the trailer and haul the floatplane to the lake. Twice this summer, Papa's backed it in the water and buzzed it around. None of the flying controls are hooked up but the rudder, so it won't fly. He's started calling them "experimental runs," and he'll write a three- or four-page notebook entry—about each one—which you can't even recognize as what happened.

"Can't you do this engine mount a little lighter?" says Uncle Hawk, rubbing his hand across it. "Get something aluminum that's just as strong as this iron piece through here?"

"I guess I could," says Papa. "What I need is bigger engines. A little more power. I know where I can get lighter engines with about twenty more horsepower, and when I get them on and hook up the flying controls she's gonna lift right up. Fly like a eagle."

Papa's still flying with Joe Ray Hoover in his Piper about two Saturdays a month, sometimes one, and keeping Joe Ray in hickory chips.

Anyway, we didn't pay much attention to Meredith and Rhonda not coming back from the graveyard until it was after dark. Nobody had seen either one of them so I drove down to the graveyard—and here's where we had the big event of the year. Meredith and Rhonda had left a note under some hedge clippers on top of Tyree's gravestone saying they'd gone to Dillon, South Carolina, to get married and would be back in two or three days.

It was such a big event it made Bliss cry.

And Papa wrote it down in one of the notebooks, with the part about the hedge clippers and Tyree's gravestone and all.

THE VINE

Walker was laid up in bed for four days with the death rattle in his chest. The grandchildren were brought in one at a time in the late afternoon to see him. The rattle could be heard through the wall. At night Caroline would heat water and wash him. She said that was all that was left to do that all else had failed. The doctor left a salve for Walker's chest and Vera brought bitters.

Two cousins John Boggs and Mantha Sutton had joined the others in the graveyard. When Walker died a new row was started with his grave and in a few days the biggest tombstone of them all was erected over it.

Years later, Caroline and her grandson Tyree died of typhoid fever. *Then Ross died of pneumonia, and on a blue moon he talked to John Boggs:*

"... and all my kids were all the time wanting to go down to see Vera because she had these here great big pockets on her apron that she kept candy in. She loved all the children, she did. She moved out of the house—about the time Helen and me started having children —into a little house me and Papa built for her down the hill.

"See, she'd put candy in them apron pockets and let the children stick their hands way down in there and find it.

"She got to be a little bit peculiar. From taking laudanum. She'd get her pension check and walk nine miles to Raleigh to get her laudanum, then come back and dance up a storm.

"Mama used to worry because she didn't seem to bathe all that much.

"She was something; didn't mind telling anybody to 'kiss her ass,' and she worried a lot about Zuba after he got strung up with the wisteria."

"That's Zuba sitting down yonder, I think," said Walker.

Ross turned and looked down toward the woods. "Well, my God it does look like him, don't it?"

"That was a bad time," said Walker.

"Yes, it was." Ross turned back from looking at Zuba.

"How's that?" asked Thomas Pittman.

"They hung Zuba," said Ross, "and we couldn't stop them. I tried. Zuba was a field hand, a nigger.

"You know, you know, Vera kept that dog and them chickens and I don't know what all right there in her house and them chickens would lay on her bed. I saw it.

"And she'd, she'd take that crazy girl from the McGuires and bring her home and let her sit and rock, and more than once I seen a chicken jump in that girl's lap and she'd stop rocking, whereas she wouldn't stop rocking for nothing else, and I went in the McGuires when that girl died—Vera was down there—and it was the oddest thing: they had a sheet over her, pinned down to every corner of the bed. I don't know whether it was because of her rocking—she'd rock no matter where she was sitting—I mean, whether they was afraid she'd start rocking after she was dead, or if she did start, or if it had something to do with their religion. They was of a unusual sect.

"You know, that girl's papa told me about Zuba's daughter and him. He told me on a wagon ride into town one time. I picked him up. It was right odd. The story was about when Zuba and his family was all still together. I remember that, when they lived back in there behind the Hughes' house—before the rest of them headed north and left Zuba. Her name was Zenobia and she had been long gone when this fellow told me about what happened. But I remembered how pretty she was, even though she was a nigger, always dressed in white, and helped her Mama clean our church. His name was Harper, first name—the one telling me. Well, Harper sort of fell in love, as it were, with Zenobia and they would meet down at Buzzard Rock, in that little cavelike space underneath. While he told me he didn't seem the least bit ashamed. She black as night and him white as cotton. He took a notion to buy her a bottle of perfume from Moses the Peddler—who I also remember; Moses brought things around in a big old wagon pulled by a little mule. It was almost Christmas and Harper was worried about if he was going to get to see her before Christmas. It was Green Woods perfume, he said, in a little bottle, and Moses had told Harper that his papa —Harper's papa—had just bought a bottle for Harper's mama for a Christmas present. Christmas came and Harper didn't get a chance to give the perfume to Zenobia, and Harper noticed his mama got only a frying pan and a mirror for Christmas, no perfume. Then when Harper met Zenobia in the little space under Buzzard Rock right after Christmas he said she smelled to high heaven—like Green Woods perfume, and it come down on him like that rock had fell in, he said, so he started following his papa on his rounds to the rabbit gums and that's where he seen them together. Then he come to find out she was pregnant, and there he was. Didn't know who was the father, him or his papa, and then the last time he saw her, she was leaving for up north in a wagon, when the whole family left except Zuba. She stopped in the store when Harper was there and motioned for him to come out to the wagon, and she showed him something: that little baby. It was black as tar, Harper said. Then somebody told Harper's papa that they'd seen Harper and Zenobia down at Buzzard Rock together, and Harper's papa beat Harper within a inch of his life, and all the while he was getting beat, Harper was saying, 'You done it, too. You done it, too.'

"He told me every word of that just like he'd been practicing telling it, and while he told it, a line of sweat broke out on his upper lip. And it was a real cool day, too."

PART THREE

1970–1971

1970

MARK

It's been unreal. It's been great. Pilot training was tough academically, but the flying was great. I got an OV-10 assignment out of pilot training—turboprop, tandem seat, fully acrobatic, over four hundred knots top speed, and I'm practically guaranteed a fighter after the year here in Thailand. I'm flying combat missions out of Nakom Phanom Air Base in northeastern Thailand. It's the real damn thing. Four-hour missions over the Ho Chi Minh Trail in Laos, looking for trucks or anything else that moves. If I find something, I call in the fighters. They come in above me, I put in a smoke rocket near the target and clear them in. They have to follow my directions. I'm a FAC—Forward Air Controller. Most of the time the target is the trail itself and half the time they miss it. But sometimes at dawn or dusk I catch trucks moving. We get our asses shot at too—looks like orange footballs coming up.

After pilot training—T-37's and T-38's—there were three

months at Travis in New Mexico—gunnery training in T-33's, old trainers really, but jets. Then three months at Ft. Walton Beach, where the honeys were thick. Travis was slow, but Ft. Walton? We had dates Thursday through Sunday nights every week. After about two weeks I met a schoolteacher, Terri Allison, and I can't say, I can't describe the times we had together. They were literally too good to be true. I'm writing her. But now there's Bangkok and it's like fifteen dollars a night at the Pardeese Hotel—for a woman. And they're all beautiful. If you get one that's ugly, you can send her back.

And I can't get over the OV-10. It's a great little aircraft. Powerful as hell, fully acrobatic, not all that complicated, a hell of a lot less complicated than the T-38.

I had about six weeks with an instructor once I got over here, on the combat missions and all that, and it was hairy. He'd be sitting behind me, and I'd forget and start flying straight and level instead of jinking and he would—and I wouldn't know this at the time—he would lift his feet up, and then slam them to the floor of the aircraft and holler through the intercom: "Goddamn, Oakley—they're shooting at us." It was wild. And then there was that first day they really did shoot at us. I was with C. C. Wasserman and he yells, "Turn *into* them, turn *into* them." He said later that if they think you see them, they'll stop shooting. Sure.

But anyway, I love it. I'm flying alone now. Before a mission, I climb up the right side, open the fuel cap on top of the wing, look at the fuel, close and check the fuel cap flush with the wing. Then I climb down and start around the aircraft. I check the right propeller for nicks and rotation; check the oil cap; pull the pin from the main gear wheel; check the strut, right main gear wheel; check the right sponson doors —closed and tight, and so on. Then I climb up and in. Airman Higgins follows me up, helps strap me in, and hands me my helmet. It's a little bit like being a king.

On the runway I line up with the centerline, hold in the brakes, open the throttles, check instruments, release the brakes. At eighty knots, I pull back the stick, rotate the nose into the air—hold it. At eighty-five knots: airborne. Hesitate, gear up. Hesitate, flaps up. Three radio calls. This is the real thing.

The cockpit fits like old soft clothes. I know the instruments and switches by heart. I wish Meredith could see me up here. What I'd really like to do is fly over where he is, and do some acrobatics. Or just run into him on an air base or something, with me wearing my survival vest. It's got a holster with a .38.

Meredith writes once every two or three weeks. He hopes I get a chance to come to Saigon instead of Bangkok. The pilots here ride a cargo plane to Bangkok for four days out of every six weeks. He says the Saigon Vietnamese are beggars and whores and thieves. Nice whores though, he says. Friendly. I know what he means. There's one place we go in Bangkok just to talk to them. They ask about pilots not there that weekend and we ask about whores not there that weekend. Just drink and talk. It's not like home, but I'm not home now.

Meredith says that fourteen guys he knows have been killed, six by mines. The last guy they sent home alive stepped in a spiked foot trap and they had to evac him with the whole thing on his foot, metal spikes out of a concrete block through his foot.

Once I'm airborne, I fly across the Mekong River, on across western Laos and into eastern Laos where I see, way down there, the Ho Chi Minh Trail: a network of roads, north-south, light orange against the dark green forests, winding like long, thin, stringy fingers, disappearing, then in the open for a distance, through mountains and flat jungle, disappearing, reappearing. The land along the roads is riddled, freckled, with bomb craters—in some places, strings of craters. Four major intersections have been bombed so bare they look like the moon. No vegetation, just sand.

When I fly reconnaisance, I hold the stick with one hand, binoculars to my eyes in the other, and look down through the Plexiglas canopy. I reverse hands—turning the aircraft gently, never flying level in a straight line. The enemy trucks, below, move north to south, south to north, usually at dawn or dusk or in the night. The big guns are camouflaged. I memorize map coordinates. I come to know intersections, river fords. I hold them in my mind almost like they are parts of my bare hand. For the longest time I did not see a person down there, until one gray morning just as it's getting light, my eyes, through binoculars, move past and then quickly back to a lone man—walking fast along the side of a road, then crossing to the other side. I watch through the binoculars from eight thousand feet up, unable to take my eyes from him. I have somehow almost believed that no humans are down there. I just find the trucks, storages, guns, river fords, and direct the air strikes. No humans are down there. Rather, some nonhuman, piranha-like force lies, swarms, sits, breeds, broods beneath the green canopy, waiting for me to fall. If we go down they chop off our heads. That's what we hear they do. And suddenly in the first gray light of day I watch this lone human being walking down a road. It is a man . . . shaped like a human being . . . walking rapidly through the gray first light. He seems soft. He is alive . . . the road another road, a country road in North Carolina and the man is someone I know; the road is a dirt road that I know with a man I know walking on it, walking on the dirt road along which he lives somewhere and the person is Meredith, Uncle Albert, Tyree, Ross, an American man from *The Grapes of Wrath*; the road a dirt road in North Carolina I've seen that man walking down a dirt road it is Lumley Road a dirt road with the gravel, the road grader has worked on it, and then, gentlemen, the body of the BLU-1/A is a hollow shell which is hinged at the base of the conical tail finassemble. The upper half acts as a lid. The filler is small, solid missiles—Lazy Dogs —having winged tail assemblies. A mechanical time fuse opens the lid, allowing immediate dispersion of the approximately 17,500 missiles, which then free fall to the target where they inflict damage by penetration. Color Code: The missile cluster adapter is painted olive drab with black markings. We also have the BLU-24/B, antipersonnel bomb sometimes called the "jungle bomb." It penetrates jungle foliage and detonates after spin is reduced below 2,000 rpm. Upon detonation, the bomb bursts and scatters cast-iron fragments in all directions. The bomb consists of a smooth cast-iron body assembly, fuse assembly, explosive train, and plastic vane assembly. When the bomb is ejected from the dispenser, the airstream reacts on the vane assembly and causes the bomb to spin. As the spin of the bomb increases, centrifugal force causes three weights in the fuse to rotate out and engage the firing pin-spring and retract the firing pin from a slide assembly which contains the detonator in an out-of-line position. The slide assembly is moved outward by centrifugal force until it is locked in place by a spring-loaded detent. The detonator in the slide assembly is now in line with the lead assembly and firing pin, and the bomb is armed. As the bomb is slowed in its fall by foliage, spin is reduced. At about 2,000 rpm, the firing pin-spring overcomes the centrifugal force of the weights, causing them to rotate inwardly until the firing pin is released. The firing pin-spring continues to act on the firing pin until the pin strikes the detonator, initiating the explosive train which bursts the body and scatters cast-iron fragments which are effective against trucks, fuel tanks, radar equipment, and personnel. Color Code: The bomb body is painted yellow with black markings. The vane assembly is ivory-colored, walking along the dirt road myself walking to the store in North Carolina myself along Lumley road to get a loaf of Merita bread and a quart of Long Meadow milk in a brown paper sack.

THE VINE

Caroline and Vera sat in the yard in the shade shelling butter beans.

I look at that trellis said Caroline and remember how Isaac and Walker argued about how wide it ought to be.

Didn't Walker come along and add onto it after Isaac finished?

Oh yes and of all the building they did that trellis is the only thing that gives clear marks of who done what.

Vera emptied shells into a basket and picked up a handful of beans from another basket. How did it happen? More handfuls.

Well I asked Isaac to build it. Don't you remember? It was about the time the field hand died. Somewhere in there is when I planted that wisteria. Got it from Mrs. Sutton and planted it early of a morning and told Isaac to build a trellis. Well when he finished Walker told him it won't big enough won't wide enough and to widen it. Isaac didn't want to do it and argued with Walker so finally Walker up and done it hisself and you can see it from the back side through the porch there where Isaac's stops and Walker's takes up.

I seen that but never remembered why it was that way.

Whoever would have thought that I'd outlive Isaac said Caroline.

I hope he died gentle.

I do too.

What if something happened to him and he went crazy and wandered off and is still alive.

Naw naw that belt buckle and them other things. They had to be right about it.

At least they wrote a letter about Seaton.

It'd been nice if we could have kept us all together out there in the graveyard.

Vera pulled unshelled beans to the top of her pile. You know Papa was right about that trellis though. It won't near wide enough.

I'm kind of glad Isaac never knew.

Never knew what?

That Walker was right.

I don't think we're going to finish these before dark.

Is that a tick on that dog's ear?

Come here Sailor.

"... and the one lost in the war," said Walker, "was Isaac."

"I tried to go in with him," said Ross, "but Mama wouldn't let me. She wrestled me down to the ground and then locked me in the

188

smokehouse so I couldn't go with Isaac, and then Isaac came to the door and told me I'd have to stay home and protect the family, which was a good thing in the end, because that's exactly what I done with the Yankees."

"How's that?"

"A bunch of Yankees come through and if I hadn't been there it's no telling what would have happened. We were working the fields and came in just before dark and there was a whole bunch of them in the backyard. They'd done stole meat and I don't know what all and. . . ."

NORALEE

I miss them both but I miss Meredith the most. He writes me about once a month. I almost got Rhonda to let me go with her to meet him in Hawaii for Meredith's R and R. But we didn't have the money.

Rhonda got pregnant while they were in Hawaii, which is great, and Meredith will be home in less than a year. I think Mark is going to stay in for twenty years. He's flying combat missions now.

In his last letter, Meredith said that he wanted to name their new baby, when it comes, Floatplane Jack or Floatplane Jane.

I'm dating this guy now that reminds me of Meredith a little bit. He's got the same curly hair and his eyes are the teeny-tiniest bit crossed, so he looks crazy sometimes. His name is Barry Hargroves and he's a senior at East Carolina. Papa saw him once, just once, and now calls him a hippie.

In his last letter, Meredith sent us these two little notices they'd just gotten. One was about leech bites. It was funny because Meredith had written on it. It said to tighten jacket cuffs to the wrists before entering streams and Meredith wrote in the margin: "Too hot for any jacket." The notice said apply insect repellant to uncovered portions of the body, and Meredith had written in: "What insect repellant?" The notice said, "If leeches are found on the body do not pull them off quickly as they will leave their heads in the bite and then cause infection." And Meredith had written: "They won't LEAVE their OWN heads, their heads will be LEFT. Ask a leech if he'll leave his head somewhere."

This was the other notice. Meredith had written "ha's" at the end of every part.

a. Remember we are guests here: We make no demands and seek no special treatment. *Ha.*

b. Join with the people: Understand their life, use phrases from their language and honor their customs and laws. *Ha Ha.*

c. Treat women with politeness and respect. *Ha Ha Ha.*

d. Make friends among the soldiers and common people. *Ha Ha Ha.*

e. Always give the Vietnamese the right of way. *Ha Ha.*

f. Be alert to security and ready to react with your military skill. *Ha Ha.*

g. Do not attract attention by loud, rude, or unusual behavior. *Ha Ha Ha Ha.*

h. Avoid separating ourselves from the people by

a display of wealth or privilege. *Wealth? Privilege? Ha.*

i. Above all else, we are members of the U.S. military forces on a difficult mission, responsible for all our official and personal actions. Reflect honor upon ourselves and the United States of America. *Ha Ha Ha.*

Meredith writes in at the end that the guy who wrote all this was the same one who thinks leeches go around leaving their heads somewhere. I show all of Meredith's letters and stuff to Barry. He just shakes his head.

BLISS

I had no idea how word would come.

I had thought about an officer in a uniform driving up to Mr. Copeland's and asking for Rhonda, a phone call to us from Mildred or Rhonda, or a telegram to Miss Esther telling her that Mark was shot down.

For some odd reason, I guess I'd never really thought about either one of them getting wounded.

It was a phone call from Rhonda, who's living with Mildred, Mr. Copeland, and Noralee:

"Bliss, Meredith has been wounded by a mine. We just got a telegram. It said it was serious. Call Thatcher and y'all come on over and I'll show you the telegram. It's just killed me. I throwed up."

I called Thatcher and he said he'd come straight home. It was something that had always been possible, but that nobody would ever talk about. Nobody around here talks about What Ifs, unless it's the weather. That's for sure.

Thatcher came in from work. "Don't they know how bad he is?" he asked as soon as he got in the door.

"All I know is what Rhonda said, that it's serious. That's all she said. She said for us to come on over there."

Thatcher rubbed his hand across the top of his head and looked around. "Well, at least he ain't dead. Let's go."

Taylor was in the backyard. I called Sylvia, my neighbor, and asked her to keep him. She said fine. We dropped him off. I didn't want him to see all of us so upset. And Meredith has been sending him presents from all over.

Mr. Copeland met us on the porch and we walked into the living room together. Mildred was sitting on the couch. Rhonda and Noralee were sitting in chairs. We walked in and Mr. Copeland stood at the door like he was waiting for somebody else. Noralee was holding the green pillow she always holds when she talks to her boyfriend on the phone. Her eyes were red. Everybody's eyes were red.

"It's right here," said Rhonda. She stood, picked up the telegram off the coffee table and handed it to me. Then she turned her pregnant self around and walked to the window and looked out.

It was the first telegram I'd ever seen, except in the movies. It said: "Staff Sergeant Meredith Copeland has been wounded in service of his country. Condition very serious but stable. Letter or phone call to follow." It had extra numbers and dates and so forth and you couldn't tell who had sent it. It was said in such a way—like a menu or church bulletin—that made me hate the paper it was on, and whoever had written it, and the Marines, and Vietnam. Meredith had been saying in his letters that one dumb man writes everything for the

Marines. I had him pictured in my head at a desk, and I felt like he had written this. It made me hate how Meredith could somehow be sucked over there, how some kind of vacuum could suck him over there to that place to have his body torn into no telling what kind of condition. Meredith.

"Maybe Mark could find out something," I said. "Miss Esther's got that phone number. She can call Mark overseas, and then maybe he can find out something. Has anybody called her?"

"We just got it—the telegram," said Mildred. "We haven't called anybody, except your house. And Albert went out to the shop and wrote it down in the notebook, I guess." She had a small towel of some sort in her hands and was wringing it. She looked at Albert. "Is that what you did, Albert?"

"Yes. I'll call Esther now," he said. He was standing by the front door, looking out, and hadn't said the first word. He went to the kitchen where the phone was and we all sat there not talking.

"Well, at least he ain't dead," said Thatcher. "He's too hard-headed for that."

We all looked at him. Thatcher seemed littler than I'd ever known him. I can't explain it. I couldn't believe that's all he could think of to say. I guess he was trying to make everybody feel better, but it didn't work.

"I just want to know what happened," said Rhonda. "How bad it is and what it is." She stood. "Y'all want something to drink?"

"I need something stiff," I said.

"Albert's got some whiskey. Everybody want some?"

"I don't," said Noralee.

Mr. Copeland, coming back in from the kitchen, met Rhonda in the doorway, stopped and backed up for her to take her pregnant self through. Then he came on in the living room. "She's coming over," he said, "and bringing Mark's phone number. We'll call him, see what he can find out."

"You can't fix no whiskey if she's coming over," said Noralee.

"That's right," said Mr. Copeland.

"Fix me one," said Mildred. "This is different, for crying out loud."

"Me, too," said Rhonda.

"Fix me one, too," I said. For everything there is a season.

NORALEE

What I thought about when I heard about it was when Meredith and I were up under the dashboard of the old DeSoto
car we had and a cramp caught him in his back and he
groaned like he was dying. I remembered it so clear. I was
around six and he was around, let's see, fourteen, and was
showing me how to hide under the dashboard and reach up
and press that button which would make the gas cap pop
open.

We had had that car for a while—it was old even back
then—and Papa ordered the electric gas cap kit out of a
book he was using to order something for the floatplane.
The ignition key had to be turned on for the button to work.
Meredith would sneak the key off the refrigerator and go
out and press that button over and over.

Then he got this idea about making money from some of
the kids in the neighborhood. They would pay him a nickel
to say "Alla Kazam" while he was pointing toward the gas cap,

which would then pop open, because I'd be lying in the front floorboard up under the dash and would reach up and press the button. It was when he was showing me how to stay out of sight, and was up under the dash himself, that the cramp caught him and I thought, for a second, that he had been electrocuted in some way and I was afraid to death he was dying.

He let Mark in on the trick and they got about four boys the first day, six or eight the second, and about fifteen the third, and were making a lot of money when Aunt Esther caught them and made them give all the money back.

But on the last day Mark hadn't made much money because Meredith had told me that when he, Meredith, coughed or sniffed after Mark said "Alla Kazam" then I shouldn't press the button. Mark got pretty frustrated.

So when the news came, that's what I thought about, and I wondered if Meredith had groaned, had rolled over groaning on the ground or what. In my mind I see all the ground over there as being dirt or mud. I can't imagine green grass. Poor Meredith.

The other main thing I thought about was that Meredith was the only one who ever carried me on his shoulders. None of the others hardly ever did and he did it a bunch. And he gave me his arrowhead collection and all his broken bats that he'd gotten from the high school team and nailed up and taped. I sold the bats for fifty cents apiece, but I've still got the arrowhead collection.

When we got the news I went in my room and called Barry and cried and cried and cried. He said he'd come over, but Aunt Esther and Bliss and Thatcher were coming so I told him to wait. Thatcher is terrible to Barry. He won't say anything to him unless it's about Canada. One of Barry's buddies went to Canada. I wish Meredith had. I swear I do.

MARK

Our barracks are in two rows, ten rooms per row, facing each other. Between them is our bar, a two-room cabin called the Nailhole. We've got a pet pig in a pen behind the Nailhole —named Napoleon. We dress him up once a week or so and let him roam around outside.

I'm walking between the barracks toward the Nailhole. It's dark, except for outside building lights. The phone beside the latrine door, next to my room, rings. A Thai boy is sitting beneath it, polishing boots. He stands, answers it. I keep walking toward the Nailhole. He lets the phone hang at the end of the cord and starts toward my room, sees me, points to the phone.

It's Mother. There's a lot of static. They got a telegram. Meredith has been wounded, seriously. Can I see what I can find out. They're real worried. I'm to call them right back if I can.

My mind jumps all around every which way. My arms start tingling and my lips feel numb.

Meredith. Wounded. Maybe it's not too bad. I call the base operator. "I need to get Da Nang. The base hospital."

I get them. "This is Lieutenant Mark, ah, Copeland at Nakhom Phanom." I'll lie. "My brother, Meredith Copeland, is there, wounded. Can you give me the name of his doctor?"

I am transferred several times and I finally get Meredith's doctor on the phone. "This is Lieutenant Mark Copeland at Nakhom Phanom. I need to find out about my brother, Meredith Copeland, who got wounded in the last day or two. I'm his brother."

I listen. He finds the file and explains that Meredith was wounded by a mine, has a head injury, and that they had to . . . oh Lord, amputate his left *arm and leg*. He asks for my number. He'll call back in a day or two if there's any change. I hang up and look at the phone. I feel sick. I think back to the last time I talked to Meredith. He had called to tell me Rhonda was pregnant.

I open the door to my room. There is this curtain of black cloth—wall to wall and ceiling to floor—in the middle of the room. Behind it are two beds. Buck, my roommate, a night flyer, is out. I close the door and flip the light switch, lighting the front half of the room. An electric clock is on my desk. It is nine thirty-five. I sit in my chair and stare at the clock. The white second hand moves through the six, the seven, the eight, the nine. My arms tingle. I've got to call home and tell them. All of them are sitting there in the living room at Uncle Albert's, or standing around the phone in the kitchen, waiting for me to call. I see Meredith swinging out over the pond on the wisteria vine; beside me in the floatplane in the shop with his navy blue ball cap pulled tight on his head the way he always wore it. I lift my arms and put them on the desk, rest my head on my arms. Meredith.

Rhonda answers. I tell her everything. No, I don't believe I want to talk to anyone else until next time. I'll call again as soon as I hear anything, but sometimes we can't get out on the phone line, and I'm really sorry about what happened, and that we'll all hope for the best. She starts crying. I look up at a floodlight, take a deep breath and think, Dear God, let him be all right and not die. We say goodbye. I hang up and walk toward the Nailhole. I'm in Uncle Albert's truck with Meredith, and he's driving across the snow on the ball field. He's skidding it all over the place. That left hand is crossing over the right one, spinning the steering wheel. His left foot is stomping the clutch pedal, and it's making that dull slam sound it always had.

I go to the wall phone in the Nailhole, find "scheduling" in the directory, call Captain Layton and explain. He says they've usually got something to be taken to Da Nang. I need to go, I say. Can he find something for me to take? He says no problem, tomorrow morning; I'll just have to check with Captain Coggins.

I go back to the bar and order a drink. Captain Whitney is talking about antiaircraft fire. "And all of a sudden an eighty-five whoofed off at about ten thou' with this great big ball of black smoke." He puts his glass on the bar and shows the size with his hands. "About that big. I said, 'Wait a fucking minute.'"

Two more pilots come in. One puts a baby duck—tan and fuzzy with brown spots—on the bar. It takes three or four steps, stops and looks around unsteadily.

I stand at the bar holding my drink. I press my palm against the cold glass.

"Whose duck?" asks Whitney.

"Ours. Bought it from a shoeshine boy—figured it'd make a good mascot. We can dress it up or something."

"We can fuck it," says Whitney. He grabs the duck and turns it upside down. Its legs stick up like short, thin pencils. He puts the duck's bottom in my face. "What is it, Oakley? Male or female? You were raised on a farm, weren't you?"

I back off, take a drink.

Whitney places the duck back on the bar near Davenport and Fletcher, who are playing cup dice. The duck runs five or six feet and stops. John, the bartender, pours water from a pitcher into a clean ashtray and places it in front of the duck. It turns and waddles away. Its wings flick when the dice cup hits the bar.

More pilots come in. One slaps a five-dollar bill onto the bar. "I got five dollars says Whitney won't bite the duck's head off."

"All right!" someone yells. "Here's a five says he will."

"You can't eat the mascot," someone says.

"Napoleon's the mascot."

"Eat Napoleon. He's getting big enough."

"Taking bets here."

John turns his back and begins washing drink glasses in soapy water.

"Bourbon and water, John."

John wipes his hands on a towel and puts ice in a glass.

"*You* bite the fucking head off the duck," says Whitney to another pilot.

I walk outside. A dull moon is low in the sky, three-fourths full—full enough to show the man in the moon looking down, surprised, open-mouthed. It's warm and breezy. Several pilots come toward me from across the lawn.

A chant rises inside the bar. "You can do it, you can do it, you can. Eat the duck! You can do it, you can do it, you can. Eat the duck!"

Then a sudden loud roar of cheers, scattered applause.

The air-conditioning in the hospital at Da Nang is out. Nobody is under covers. My father died in a hospital like this. I wonder if it was hot, or cool, or cold. A medic is taking me to Meredith. He tells me Meredith can't talk. Can't *talk*. We enter a ward. I scan and find the one with his left leg and arm missing. He is asleep in plain green bed clothes. Bottles hang on racks. Tubes are in his nose. The medic stops and points at him. At first I don't recognize his face. I read the name on the foot of the bed to be sure: Meredith Ross Copeland, E-3, USMC. The medic leaves. Meredith's left arm and leg are only half there, stubbed, bandaged, white. His pale, almost yellow face is turned to the side, the top and left side of his head bandaged, his mouth open, lips swollen. Dark brown circles are under both eyes, his right hand drawn, drawn in toward his side—like the arm of someone who has had a stroke.

I turn and walk away so I can get my breath.

I turn back around and start toward Meredith, then stop. He can't talk. If he wakes up, I will be drawn down into his eyes. I will be turned upside down, held there and shaken and turned sideways and spun, so I turn my back on him and walk away to make it through this myself, now. I stop and look up into a light in the ceiling, and a boy in a bed says, "He ain't going to make it, sir. Me and Danny over there already got money on it."

I walk out of the room and into a hall. I can't remember which way to turn. I walk through an exit door into the sunshine. A wheelchair sits out there, beside a wooden bench. Nobody is around. The sunlight catches on one of the wheelchair spokes, and it glints like a tiny sustained bolt of lightning.

THE VINE

William who was Walker and Caroline's last born went out every morning to check his rabbit boxes. Zuba the second field hand a black man got him started on all that built boxes for him spent time with him until William began to fret getting tired of Zuba's attention. Sometimes William would bring the rabbits home live in a potato sack and kill them against the smokehouse. He'd hold a rabbit by its hind legs whirl it round and round over his head and then bang its head against the corner of the smokehouse. Zuba would come out it would be very early in the morning and fuss at him take the rabbit away from him and give it a rabbit punch because the rabbit would not be dead yet. To kill it William's way took many bangs against the corner of the smokehouse.

William began to bring things home and keep them alive which was uncommon except in the normal case of a possum which would be kept in a barrel and fed good food for a few weeks. Then he'd be killed cleaned cooked and eaten.

When the possum barrel was empty and William came home with a rabbit in his sack sometimes he would put the rabbit in the possum barrel and late at night he would come out of the house get the rabbit take it behind the smokehouse and do something to it. Once Caroline found a rabbit dead with its front teeth pulled.

Then William gave up his rabbit boxes altogether and began to bring home larger trapped animals. Walker beat him for skinning a fox while it was alive.

Then William moved into town and after the sun was up one morning and the family was in the field he rode into the yard in a wagon pulled by a mule. He got down off the wagon looked around took something heavy in a big tow sack up out of the wagon walked the few steps with it to the smokehouse placed it on the ground then pushed it with his hands up underneath the edge of the smokehouse as far as it would go. He then pushed it farther with his feet. He stood and fetched a hoe from the corncrib and with the blade end of the hoe pushed the sack and whatever was in it farther under the smokehouse.

Ross was returning by the pond from the corn field. He stopped and watched.

William got in the wagon and left.

Ross walked into the yard squatted and looked under the smokehouse went into the kitchen then returned to the field.

That night two wagonloads of men rode into the yard. They carried pine torches for light. William and a black woman were with them. They swarmed to the smokehouse door and pulled Zuba out. The black woman stood back. Zuba was the field hand once a slave freed after the war who lived in the smokehouse and worked for food only. They tied his hands behind his back and set him on the back porch steps. Several of them then pushed into the smokehouse then back out and around behind it. William stood back. One squatted put his hand to the ground bent over lowered his torch and then called to the others. Walker Caroline Vera Ross and Helen stood on the back porch watching. Walker held a lantern. He set it on the porch. Zuba looked up at him the flame reflecting against his wet face.

They dragged the sack out and pulled back its lip. There was hair the color of yellow flowers.

One of the men screamed and dropped to his knees as if hit by a sledge hammer. He got to his feet and ran at Zuba jumped on him hitting pounding with his fists making flat pounding sounds of skin against skin. Zuba tried to turn away. Several of them pulled the man off finally. Another man wearing a black coat asked Walker to bring out a table. Walker stood there. Caroline held his arm.

Ross dug at his thumb nails with his middle fingernails. Blood came.

The man with the black coat went into the kitchen and came out with a small table. The torches cast shadows against the kitchen the house the smokehouse. The man in the black coat asked for a Bible. William went inside and brought one out stopped on the porch and spoke to Caroline and Walker explaining. The man placed the Bible on the table and asked William to place his hand on it. He asked questions and William talked. Two others talked and then the black woman. The man said Zuba was guilty of murder. As three men came to get him Zuba fell back against the steps moving as if he were trying to go through them and into the ground. Walker almost seventy stooped pale weak started down the steps. He moved among them trying to stop them then pulled at the man wearing the black coat pulling the coat off the man's shoulder exposing a suspender strap over a white shirt. The man pulled away and Walker was at last held back by two boys.

They dragged Zuba to and up into the wagon. The man in the black coat asked Walker for rope but Walker didn't move or talk. A man started to cut a rein from the horses at the wagon. William pointed toward the pond and said The wisteria vine. A single strand hung from a tree. Children used it to swing out over the pond and drop in. In a crowd the men all moved to that strand of vine pulling Zuba sitting in the middle of the wagon the torches moving together bouncing fire. Walker called his family inside where they all went except for William.

A man fashioned a noose out of the vine and a belt and placed it around Zuba's neck. Then another man whipped the horses so that the wagon was pulled from beneath Zuba and they all watched his legs flail so that he turned around and around and around. Afterwards several remained cut him down went to the back door of the house talked to Walker dug a grave in the woods near the family graveyard finishing deep in the night and buried him after roosters were crowing.

MEREDITH

I dreamed I saw Mark walk out of this ward, on out that door. He was wearing a flight suit. And across the room, that stupid asshole that keeps saying I'm going to die, he said they had money on it—that I won't going to make it.

There's a leg and arm been knocked out—knocked off —but there's a good, alive great big peach pit in me somewhere, about the size of a baseball, that ain't going nowhere. And the doctor told me I was going to make it. He said all my vital signs are strong, but there's a head-wound problem, giving me paralysis, and a talking problem.

I don't remember what happened, but some of them have been in and told me. Starnes come by a couple of days ago . . . or, I can't remember his name, and told me that Hux and Mattherson and Hickman were all killed. He looked pretty shook. Hux. Hux is toughest to think about. Hux was my buddy.

If I could talk I'd tell that son of a bitch across the way to keep his goddamn mouth shut and I'd get somebody to set his fucking mattress on fire. There's plenty of guys in here would do it. Burn his ass up. Ass his burn up. Something.

What is odd is that I ain't felt a lot of pain yet, except my ear mainly. It's all numb—the ends of my leg and arm. My head. The doctor told me I'd get some odd sensations. I do grip things with my left hand—the one that's gone. I grip. I look down there, like I'll look down there right now. I look down there and see where the bandages end. And beyond that in the air I grip with my hand. I grip onto something. Anything that I want to think about, I grip onto. Usually it's a cold metal bar and I can feel the cold in my hand. And I read the newspaper in my head. It'll come up in my mind and I read it but it don't make no sense. I can't stop it from happening, and there are all kinds of things I can't remember.

What I wish is there was some way I could grab my dick, which thank God is all there.

It was the realest dream I've ever had. Mark just walking, stopping, looking up at that light, walking out the door with jerkhead over there mouthing off.

God knows I could've died. And I'd end up at the graveyard. It's in my papers and I wrote it to Bliss in a letter and talked to her about it, and told the others. Bliss would make them do it. Whatever there was of me left would be in the graveyard.

We picked pieces of bodies off a fence one time. I got a piece we couldn't tell was a big elbow or a little knee.

What a dicked-up thing. It's like what Hux wrote on his helmet—SHIT HAPPENS. What I'm glad about is I got my brain, mostly. I can think, but you get shrapnel in your head, man.

Lead head. Now whatever used to be there to pull the words out of my head and stick them in my mouth to spit out —whatever that was—is gone. Adios. So I get the words and stick them in a wheelbarrow and start walking forward with them and they roll over this cliff into nothing, into thin air, and if it's the doctor listening, he's okay; he carries a piece of paper with "yes" on one end, "no" on the other end, and "maybe" in the middle. And I can look at the word I want. He says it's good I'm continent. That means I can shit and piss on my own. Lucky me. A cow bends her back when she pisses, curved like a new moon.

I get a hard on in the night and want to jack off, but I can't.

Rhonda ain't going to be happy just jacking me off. And she ain't going to stand for me just sitting around, shitting in a pan. I know that. We'll have to figure out something. But whatever we figure out, I feel it in my bones that she'll skip.

One thing, I ain't going to be in the field again. I ain't going to eat no more C-rations; see nobody blown up with red and blue insides hanging out; ain't going to see no more leeches; and neither one of my tattoos got blown away.

The worst thing is not being able to talk. I'd rather be blind, and get around, than like I am now. I'd rather be anything but dead than the way I am right now, except if I couldn't think straight. I can't think straight, exactly, all the time. But that don't bother me. You don't have quite so much to think about if you can't go nowhere.

I'm getting letters from everybody, and Aunt Esther has got them writing from the church. The Red Cross volunteer who brings them to me is about the same age as Bliss and she's from Tennessee and the way she talks, her accent—she's mighty good looking too—makes my blood run hot.

Blood blockage in the brain. Can you believe the good luck in that? I get a arm and a leg blown away and why couldn't that be the side that gets paralyzed? Why not? Six, half a dozen. Seems like a good God could have done that.

Bliss tried to tell me. She was the only one. I wish I *had* gone to Canada. I could be in Canada in a cool breeze, swimming. There are plenty of fools ready to get blown apart for what they believe in about this mess over here. The hell they are. Nobody's ready to get blown apart. The only reason they do it is they know they're not going to get blown apart. I knew better than anything I won't going to get blown apart. I would have bet my life on a butcher block.

Every morning when I wake up I try to remember the day it happened and I can't, so I try to remember one day in my life at home. I get a piece of it, like me and Mark frog-gigging, or hunting at Uncle Hawk's, or playing ball, and I try to remember everything in that piece of day. I put it all together, little piece by little piece. I hold it there and get the pieces together like a puzzle, then I run my fingers smooth over the pieces four or five times and by then breakfast is over—a nigger feeds me—and Miss Clairmont is on the way with a big smile and letters and she takes her time with me, like she's got all day. I want her to take her hair down so bad I don't know what to do. I could eat every inch of her with the half of my mouth that works. Yankee Doodle.

THATCHER

Meredith got his arm and leg blowed off by a tank mine. All we can do is thank God he didn't get killed. Two guys I went to high school with have gotten killed. Sam Bartlett and Alton McAllister. They were good guys, too. I looked up their pictures in the yearbook to see what sports they were in. Sam Bartlett wadn't in the first thing. There was just his name there.

Bliss is beside herself—standing at the window looking for the mailman. Mark sends a postcard or letter everytime he hears from Meredith's doctor.

Rhonda is jumpy. Pregnant, throwing up, and crying at everything. She had to stop singing in her rock-and-roll band and God knows I'm surprised she didn't have an abortion so she could keep singing. Bliss said they shouldn't have gotten married and she was right. Meredith needed to be about forty before he got married.

And Papa has started working on the floatplane again. It

was disassembled and piled in the back of the shop but now he's got it all back together again. The notebooks he's kept going. He's got all the stuff we've heard from Meredith in there. He says the first thing he's going to do when Meredith gets home is give him a ride on the lake. Good luck. He may give him a ride on the lake, but not in the air. He's on his third set of engines and there's no way that damn thing will ever fly. It's too ugly for one thing.

He ought to be spending some time working on Noralee's ass. She's dating a hippie and word was, a couple of years ago, that she had the hots for a nigger. It's like she's just hanging around, soaking up how things are going crazy, especially with all this marching against the war. I sure as hell can't talk to her, and I thank my lucky stars that Taylor ain't but seven —with all this crap going on.

I've got Taylor hitting left-handed like Papa tried to do with Mark and Meredith. He helps me wash the car too. And I got him shooting a rifle.

Me and Bliss had a big fight about him shooting the rifle, but hell, it don't kick. A rifle don't kick.

Bliss is odd that way. I think this whole thing about Meredith and Mark going off to war influenced her somehow. She's touchy about stuff. And now with Meredith getting his arm shot off and all, she's more jumpy than ever.

MEREDITH

The flight from 'Nam seemed like around the world. I was on a stretcher and couldn't sit up. Straight out as the ace of spades. A lot of other guys were on the plane, too. Except most of them could sit up. And sip soup.

This is one goddamn hell of a big mess, and I'll be in one goddamn hell of a big mess for the rest of my life, and I don't know why somebody couldn't have sat down and figured something out over there, beforehand. If they all had to go through this theirselves or either figure out how to stop it, then it would have stopped because nobody is going to choose to go through this kind of goddamned worthless condition. But the Communists won't compromise is what they say. Them little shits are tough. I know that. The oddest thing is seeing a head gone and just a Adam's apple left. We shot one with a pocket full of letters. Hell, I don't know what to think. It pisses me off worse than I can even feel, and if I could talk I couldn't say it, because my

216

voice could never get loud enough to yell it as loud as I'd want to.

I might can walk in a year, they said. It don't feel like it now. I'll have to get an artificial bank. Lank. Bank.

Across the Pacific seemed like forever, but from Randolph to Fayetteville, which is a whole lot shorter, seems twice as long. For one thing we've stopped four times. It's like a carrot in front of a donkey. It keeps pulling away.

At least this time I'm in a wheelchair. Those stretchers suck. There's an Air Force airman who's in charge of three of us. The other two are in a hell of a lot better shape than me, so the airman spends most of his time with me.

We all three have got our uniforms on.

I got a Purple Heart. And two purple nubs.

When the feeling started coming back, they stung and tingled like crazy, and people look at you like what's wrong with you. But I figured out the way to do it is don't try to talk unless you've practiced something over and over because you try to say it and can't, you come across real stupid. It comes out like a goose barking sometimes. It's like you can't control it.

They got my coat sleeve and pant leg pinned up nice. They got a little book on all this for AMPUTEES. Man, I've thought that word a thousand times, and I ain't got the nerve to try to say it.

So they got this little book for all the Mr. Nubs. It shows you a couple of ways to fix your shirts, jackets, pants. I'll have to do it the easy way: put my jacket sleeve in my pocket. Rhonda don't sew. And the book goes into all this stuff about artificial limbs. It says that for most people, artificial arms never work out, and only about half the ones that need it end up with an artificial leg. The rest rather do without it. I ain't made up my mind. I'll have to see what I think.

There's going to be a therapist for me at home and all that, and I'll be able to try out several different styles of artificial limbs in about two months. Something I look forward to.

I got my voice back and I can say a few words. I got a little movement in my right shoulder and right hip.

I had one wet dream, and when they cleaned me up I didn't give a shit because it was worth it. One thing I could use is a warm, soft hand down there. Jackie, jackie, jackie, jackie, jackie.

The problem with me screwing Rhonda is that Rhonda will have to screw *me* and how the hell are you supposed to hold onto somebody with a nub and a paralyzed hand. Grip her shoulders? This is going to be a tough part of readjustment. That so-called counselor at Da Nang was in the wrong tree. He talked about all the wrong stuff. Emotional adjustment and all that. I ain't worried about the emotional stuff. Frankenstein. I'm worried about jacking off, or somebody else jacking me off, and fucking; and I'm worried about when Rhonda's going to leave, before or after the baby's born, and I'm worried about how I'm going to look like I'm supporting a family; the government is supposed to take care of that, thank God; and one of the things that galls me and scares me is holding the baby. Without dropping him, or her, whichever: Floatplane Jack, Floatplane Jane. What kind of daddy am I going to be? Whoopee. Time to play catch, time to play marbles, time to jump rope, time to talk, sing cowboy songs. Oh, bury me not on the lone prairie.

It's amazing how much time you get to think when you can't talk or go nowhere. And you start to figure out what life is, which is doing things. Things you've already done, or are getting ready to do. Like I am, you can't do nothing but think. If I can ever get to the place I can drive, then I can buy some kind of van with a lift. They had them in the pamphlet, too.

The plane engines are cut back; we're floating into Fayetteville. This thing hadn't got any windows so I can't look out at the trees. There's a knot been coming up in my throat. The pilot announced North Carolina. Damn if I want to start crying. It's going to be Rhonda, Mama, Papa, and Thatcher picking me up, and the rest will be waiting at home. My home dog, Fox, died. He was too old. Papa had him put to sleep. Bliss has wrote me more than Rhonda has.

My shoe—Johnny One-Shoe—is spit-shined. I look pretty good actually, considering.

We touch down, hard. Taxi. This knot in my throat. We stop. The ramp in the back of the plane is lowered. The Air Force guy rolls me out, slower than he needs to. There are other Army guys coming on board to roll some of the others out. There's a strong breeze. My hat's in my lap. We're rolling across the ramp, toward the terminal. No bands. I see people through the glass. Not Rhonda, Mama, Papa, Thatcher. But they're there, I know. Shit, I'm losing it. I'm going to be crying like a baby. No loud noises, please. I'm going to be crying like a baby. I hate it. They might as well be carrying me in a goddamned cradle. Rock-a-bye baby, in the tree top. When the wind blows, the cradle—

In through the doors. I straighten up.

There they are. Rhonda in a white dress. She's gained

weight. Besides in her stomach. Her face. I say out loud to myself: "Hi, Babe."

Here they come. I practice: "Hi, Babe. Hi, Babe." God, Rhonda's crying, too. Thatcher, shit, Thatcher looks like he has every day of his life. Mama looks great. Papa looks old, tired.

Rhonda's arms come out toward me. Okay—loud, loud and clear:

"Hi, Bake." Goddamn it.

Oh, her arms.

Tight. No, no, LONGER. I WANT YOU TO HOLD ME A MINUTE. Standing back now in that white dress. And Thatcher standing there patting me on the shoulder. I can't get the arm up yet.

Papa.

I work it up from the upper stem of my spinal cord, through my tongue and spit it out: "Papa."

He reaches down and grabs my hand. Shit, he's crying, face all jerked around. I try to squeeze back. Useless.

Mama gives me the longest hug, and she says something in my ear but I don't understand it. I think about asking her to say it again but I can't.

Thatcher rolls me. Rhonda walks on one side, Mama on the other, Papa behind. The Air Force guy, I'd forgot him, is carrying both my bags. The other two fellows, I wanted to say bye to them. I got "bye" down pretty good.

They roll me out into the parking lot. The bright sunlight does funny things to my right eye. Try to explain that when you can't talk. ". . . the sunshine in. Take it with a grin."

Thatcher takes my bags from the Air Force guy—who's

got leave now. He told me on the trip. He's going home to his girlfriend, and his boat, and his '62 Chevrolet, and his daddy's sheep farm, and three shotguns, and a rifle, and a guitar. "Bye," I say in my Golden Tone.

We roll up to the jeep. Same old goddamn jeep. And a dog. Oh yeah. Mark's new dog, but I can't remember his name.

Son of a bitch if Papa ain't put a shell over the truck bed and he's—damn if he ain't rigged it for head room, and him and Thatcher's pulling out two boards, and they got a *rope* and—shit, watch this:

Papa ties the rope to the front of the wheelchair, between my legs—leg. Get it in the center, Papa. I'll guarantee you nobody in the U.S. Marines today calls their papa Papa except me.

Thatcher is behind me. Papa gets up into the truck bed, holding the rope. They start me up. I look over at Rhonda and Mama standing there. Two or three other people have walked up, a soldier too, and are looking. The soldier is looking at Rhonda. Rhonda and Mama are looking a little worried about me making it. Well, what the hell might happen? I might break my goddamned arm or something. I might FALL for Christ's sake, and break my goddamned arm—whoa —and THEY MIGHT SEND ME TO VIETNAM. This is a major risk operation. I wish I could holler. I wish I could holler that it's good to be home, even with old Thatcher around. Glory be.

Shit, that was pretty easy. They turn me around and back me up against the bed and fasten the back of the wheelchair to the damn truck bed—something Papa rigged. Right on, man. If I were a carpenter and you were a baby. Or something. And Rhonda's got a lawn chair back here and is going to sit with me on the way home. Shit, Rhonda, you'd be riding with that goddamned sergeant if things were a little different.

While we ride, I spend most of my time looking at Rhonda and her fat stomach. Cars come up behind us and people look in.

Rhonda tells me over and over that they got a banner and everything for me at home. And that I look good.

I dreamed I was home in the graveyard twice, and then that dream about Mark that was the realest I ever had.

The cab shell has got crank-out windows. I watch Rhonda and then the pine trees. It's pretty noisy to talk. I can't hear her sometimes. The dog is laying down nice. Rex, that's his name. Fox died.

We turn in the driveway, and then Papa backs out into the road and turns the truck around and backs in the driveway and across the lawn right up to this sign: a sheet drooped over a badminton net that says WELCOME HOME MEREDITH.

It's real good to be here, but I want to jump out and hug everybody, and go out to the dog pen and yell at the dogs.

There they all are—standing at the steps. There's Bliss. Who is—Noralee? God, she's a hippie. Good for her. I bet old Thatcher's pissed.

Bliss. Bliss has got that look on her face. Bliss could take care of me forever and wouldn't think twice about it.

Aunt Esther. Corncob up her ass like always. Damn if she ain't crying too. Whoopee. Oh, God, get me through this. Where am I going to live and who with? Bury me not.

Look at them new yellow-wood ramps. Papa is at it again.

Inside, Aunt Esther has these pictures of Mark and his

airplane. That's wonderful. Wonderful, wonderful Mark.

I try not to talk any more than I have to. I can shake my head yes and no, push up my shoulder for maybe. I don't want to say what I ain't practiced. The therapist is supposed to come this afternoon.

What I'd like to know is what happened to God. Aunt Esther, you got him locked up somewhere, afraid to let him out—afraid he might hear somebody cussing, for Christ's sake? If that's the way it works He ain't ever been in a war. And you figure in a posse of twelve fishermen, you're going to have some nasty language. That's the part that gets left out. Boy, if they knew I'd smoked dope. WHOA. But some of the church women wrote me nice long letters. I got to give them some credit. Credit where credit's due.

And here comes Thatcher with a puppy, a damn bird dog puppy, lemon and white, with a damn red ribbon. Bliss done the ribbon.

"His name's Floatplane," Rhonda says.

They put him in my lap and he's up licking my neck, wagging his tail. Shit, I'm losing it again.

Papa ain't going to allow no dog in the house over a minute.

They have my favorites for supper—T-bone steak, french fries, apple pie and ice cream. Rhonda feeds me. I got a little baby bib and everything. That was in the packet they sent home with me. Rhonda don't seem to mind. But this ain't Rhonda, friends. This ain't going to be her style for very long.

They talk about the trip, the packet, and all it says about getting me in bed.

Then the therapist comes and explains. He's nice. He explains stuff about the shit pan, and getting me in bed and all that, and then leaves. They all ask me some yes and no questions. I'm Mr. Congeniality or whatever it is. Hi Bake.

After supper, Bliss is squatting down, talking to me straight on. She hugged me long and tight, like Mama. She will always hug me long and tight.

Aunt Esther is already gone. She was pretty shook.

Thatcher pats me on the shoulder. "That hurt, boy?"

I shake my head. HELL NO, THATCHER, IT'S A REGULAR GODDAMN NORMAL SHOULDER. IT DON'T HURT ANYMORE THAN NORALEE'S OVER THERE. THE HURT IS OVER. HIT ME ANYWHERE. YOU DUMMY.

He bends over a little bit, and says loud, like I'm deaf, "I'm glad you're back in one piece."

SHIT ALMIGHTY. I AIN'T BACK IN ONE PIECE, THATCHER. THERE ARE SEVERAL OTHER PIECES. SHIT. ONE PIECE? THE REST OF ME IS COMING HOME U.P.S. YOU AIN'T CHANGED A BIT, THATCHER.

I give him the shrug.

If Mark had Thatcher's stupidness and Thatcher had Mark's sissiness, they'd be even.

I got a brace for the good leg—or for the leg, period. I got a brace for the leg and that gets clicked out straight and two of them get under my arms and stand me up and I always get dizzy and everything whites out and nobody ever gives me a chance to settle down before they sit me down on the bed, so I don't get a chance to enjoy standing up very much. The bandages are off my head. My hair's growing back. Fuzzy Wuzzy was a bear. My ear drains a little. Neat.

So now here are me and Rhonda in bed and I can feel this

ain't going to work out. I don't know how I feel it, but I know, because I know Rhonda. It would work out with somebody like Bliss. Rhonda loves to sing better than anything and is afraid of being stuck with Mr. Nub, and Mr. Nub's baby, and laying here in bed with a man that can't talk, can't walk, can't hardly move, can't jack off, can't eat, could kiss a little bit if she'd move on over and get close. But that would just set her up for nothing, and I swear I don't believe she's going to do one damn thing but close her eyes and go to sleep.

On the third night home, Papa gets this idea to take me out and set me in the floatplane. This is after the therapist come again and explained my exercises to Rhonda and Mama. Rhonda hadn't been too sick lately, with the pregnancy. She's doing real good, Bliss says. She's working at the auto parts store and hates it worse than anything. I don't know how she got a job there, I swear I don't. She don't know a wheel from a radio aerial, but it's less than a mile away and she can come home for lunch, and the guy lets her come home when she feels bad.

But I see all this ain't going to work out too good. I'm one goddamned whole hell of a lot of trouble. I've got to work my ass off on the exercises so I can start taking care of myself. Mama and Rhonda are going to alternate days this first week. Bliss is going to help out the second week.

Anyway, Papa came home for lunch while the therapist was here, and of course had to take him out to the shop and show him the floatplane. They pushed me out there. The therapist thought it was some kind of swampboat until Papa opened the wings out.

So that night, my third night home, papa decides he wants me to sit in the floatplane. Okay, I'll sit in the floatplane. I don't mind. I figure it's SOMETHING.

Mama didn't like the idea at all but Papa says they can use the pulleys to get me up in the seat—that it'll be easy. Mama says it's dangerous, but I'm thinking it ain't dangerous. What's the worst that can happen?—I bust my ass?

Everybody gets in the act except Noralee, who is gone off with this guy who came to get her and wouldn't even get out of his car when he drove up.

Thatcher rolls me out to the shop and everybody follows. We roll into the shop, which has that same sawdust, electric-saw smell it's always had, and there that thing sits like some kind of giant red mosquito.

It's up on two long tables—it won't fit on the floor with all the crap in there—so they can't stand me up and then sit me down in it like if it was on the floor. They got to use Papa's idea: pulleys. The pulleys are hooked to two rafters, and Papa's got Noralee's old swing seat hooked at the low end of the chains.

Mama has given up on complaining about it and is standing there beside me, ready to hold my shoulders. There is a ladder for her to climb up same time I go up.

I'm waiting to see what's going to fall—first.

Somebody lets Floatplane in. He knocks something over. "Get that dog out of here," says Papa.

Mama is still worried: "Albert, I don't know about this. At least check it out somehow first to see if that pulley's going to hold him."

"Thatcher, come here." Papa grabs the swing seat. It's about chair bottom level up from the floor. The chains are hooked in the rafters directly above the cockpit and swerve down beside the cockpit toward the floor.

"Wait. Here, let's slide the floatplane out of the way," says Papa. "We'll pull him straight up, slide it under him, and then drop him down into the cockpit."

I force it out: "DROP?!"

They laugh, and slide the tables and plane out of the way as far as they will go.

"I mean, *ease* you down," says Papa. "Thatcher, here. Sit in here for a minute."

"What for?"

"I just want to see—for Mildred—that it'll hold him."

Thatcher sits. The rafters creak a little.

"See," says Papa to Mama.

"I think you ought to check, see if it'll lift him up a little ways," says Mama.

"Okay. Okay." Papa pulls on one pulley, then the other; one, then the other; so that Thatcher is level, then slanted one way, level, then slanted the other way.

"See," says Papa, and releases one side all the way so that Thatcher has to grab the chains at the same time his feet drop.

Papa rolls me over to the chains, unhooks the swing seat from the chains, slips the swing seat up under me and hooks the chains to the swing seat.

"Let's pull up both sides even," says Thatcher.

They start me up, with Mama beside me holding my shoulders so I can keep my balance. "Lean back, son, I got you."

I'm thinking, If I pitch forward . . . the damn floor down

there is concrete. If I pitch forward, my ass is dead.

They get me up there. Mama has to go up a couple of steps on the ladder. She's beside me, holding me so I keep my balance. I'm able to do a good job with my arm nub, holding the chain against my side.

Papa and Thatcher and Bliss get the tables and the floatplane under me so that the left lawn chair in the cockpit is directly below me, then they start easing me down, finally into the chair. Damn aluminum lawn chair bolted in there. That's the damn ejection seat in this thing.

I look around. It's almost the very same as when me and Mark used to sit in it. And of all the days I've been patching together like little puzzles to run my fingers over, I'd forgotten the ones when we'd sit out here in the floatplane and go on bombing missions over Germany and Japan and Korea. Five, four, three, two, one . . . .

I think about us sitting out here, and then getting down out of the floatplane and doing things in the shop—with both hands, then going outside and running, and running, and running, and running, tackling each other, getting my nose hit so my eyes water and I sneeze.

Something about all that, something almost like a blanket, falls down over my head and shoulders and I start crying, my head drops and I start crying like a baby and they all think I'm crying because I don't want to be in the floatplane, but I *do* want to be in the floatplane. I want to remember and feel it all, to dream it up, to see me and Mark sawing some shape out of plywood or making our own kite—with our own sticks made from bamboo reeds, or making a glass-covered box for arrowheads, and then going out to look up at a white and blue sky, and go running and running and running off down to the woods somewhere.

But they all start doing everything they can to get me down, getting the pulley hooked back up, Mama back up the ladder. I want them to get out of the shop, to leave me alone and let me put together one of those days like it happened, like a puzzle, and run my fingers over it, but I have to relax and let them do all they have to do—over and under me like ants hauling a dead roach off somewhere, back inside to get put to bed and listen to Rhonda think about what in God's name she is supposed to do with me in bed.

It's pretty crowded in the house here. We've got to figure something out. Mama wants to build on a new bathroom, but Papa says we don't need it.

Papa does his share. I can say that. He usually helps me get in the tub every few nights. The worse part is somebody helping me take a shit and then wiping my ass. Rhonda did that for awhile pretty regular, but she's starting finding more and more to do come shit time. Papa don't mind. Papa is like a woman in some ways. He don't mind a lot of stuff.

He took me hunting on the first morning of hunting season. We didn't stay the whole day, and I just sat in the truck, but it was good to get out. I slept on the couch so I wouldn't wake Rhonda up. Papa came in and woke me up and put on my leg brace, clicked it out straight and stood me up. I can grip pretty good with my right hand now. I stand in a walker to get dressed. I been thinking about how I'd be getting around now if it hadn't been for the brain thing—I'd be able to do everything by myself. When I start thinking about that

I get depressed sometimes. Growing up, I never got depressed; I don't know anybody who did. I didn't even hardly know what it was until that jerk counselor in Da Nang started talking about it. Somebody hired him in California and sent him to Vietnam to talk to the ones blowed up bad. Bad mistake. But I do get depressed now, if I start thinking about now. I can think about days when I was growing up and that helps me to feel good for some reason. At least I don't get depressed. But if I think about now, or the future, with Rhonda gone—I can really tell she's going to be gone, and I'm glad in a way because I worry about it all the time—it's pretty easy to get depressed, a real heavy feeling when you don't want to do anything, not even think. The halls of winter. It's like I'm walking around in dark halls.

But I got an electric typewriter now on a little hospital eating table that can be rolled anywhere. I can't reach up and do letters yet, but Papa engineered this metal arm with a crook in the end where it hits the keys and another metal arm hooked to that that I can hold in my hand. It's got a gear and a roller so that without much movement I can cover all the keys. Somebody's just got to keep paper in the thing. And I've subscribed to a airplane magazine and I'm going to start collecting instructions for home-built aircraft. It's sort of a joke because Papa has never had all the instructions to the floatplane. I'm going to start collecting—I don't know what kind yet. I sure as hell can't get instructions for our floatplane—not a full set, not from the shop.

Anyway, on the hunt, first day of hunting season, Papa rolled me in and cooked a big breakfast, sang a few songs like Uncle Hawk, and told me that great story about when they were in school and the teacher, who they called Mr. Yellow because he was so pale, made Uncle Hawk stick his head in the trash can for tying the bell up so it wouldn't ring. Uncle Hawk says, "It stinks in here," and the teacher kicked the trash can and Uncle Hawk forgot he was under a table and jerked his head out of the trash can and banged it against the bottom of the table. Papa said Led Cross had remembered it all his life and mentioned it every time he saw Uncle Hawk. That got me to thinking about the Florida trips. Mark will be home on leave this Christmas, and we'll all go to Florida together again. Strike up the band.

Papa still writes stuff in the floatplane notebooks. He showed it to me. He's got everything in there about the floatplane, and more. He scotch-taped this newspaper clipping in there about getting the truck out of the pond, the time I drove it in there. I'd forgot it was written up in the newspaper. *Hanson County Pilot,* June 13, 1958. That was twelve years ago—long enough to get an education.

THE LISTRE REPORT

BY

MRS. GARLAND LUCAS

LISTRE—Those who have traveled in our local woodlands have no doubt had occasion to traverse past the old Copeland family graveyard with its attendant pond and acre-covering wisteria vine—all on the old Listre-Bethel Road, now closed.

Albert Copeland had a unique problem to solve yesterday at his pond. His truck was underwater in the deep end, yes the deep end. Mr. Copeland, who built bridges and served as a frogman in World War II, we have been told, and now manages the Anderson Sawmill, walked into the pond in his bathing suit with a cinderblock tied to his ankle. Attached to his nose was a clothespin. What an interesting sight to this reporter! On his eyes were swimming goggles, and in his mouth was the end of a long green garden hose, held there by his hand. Mr. Copeland's other hand held the chain to be hooked to the truck's rear axle. Esther Oakley, Mr. Copeland's sister, also of Listre, held the other end of the hose while standing on shore. All of this provided yesterday for much local excitement.

The submerged truck had been located underwater and marked with an anchored balloon. After a few minutes out of sight, Mr. Copeland surfaced holding his fingers in a victory sign, having untied the cinderblock from his ankle. He then swam to shore where he directed the rescue of his truck—yet another step in the unfolding drama.

Thatcher Copeland, heavy equipment operator with Strong Pull Construction Company, Inc., and son of Mr. Copeland, drove the bulldozer which pulled the truck up out of the pond. However, the recovery was not without complications, as readers will soon see.

The bulldozer had to be driven down the dam in order to pull the truck up out of the pond. Mr. Copeland found it necessary to construct a fulcrum of sorts, a wood pile, over which the chain could ride. Then oil was poured onto the chain as it was pulled across the wood. Mr. Copeland explained that the oil reduced friction in a way which facilitated the operation. The truck was indeed pulled up out of the water and onto the dam and eventually towed to Lawrence Wilson's Texaco where the engine will soon be overhauled. "I was planning to overhaul the engine anyway, and it hadn't been underwater long enough for rust to set in," explained Mr. Copeland, who said that the success of the operation was due to "friction reduction" and "natural suspension." When asked how the truck came to be in the pond in the first place, he responded, "No comment."

A crowd, including the mayor of Listre, Steelman Crenshaw, attended the event.

Lotis Durham, a foreman with Strong Pull Construction Company, arranged for use of the bulldozer. Mr. Durham, also present at the event, said that Strong Pull, Inc., has an interest in various and varied kinds of community projects.

Mr. Crenshaw will also be at the Kiwanis Barbecue Supper next Saturday, June 21. Everyone is invited to support this worthwhile project, the proceeds of which will be for the Friends of the Library as well as for handkerchiefs, combs, and toilet articles for the young men at the YMRC.

This concludes your Listre Report.

Papa had underlined the part about natural suspension. What "natural suspension" is is nothing but this giant mystery. And what Papa does is figure out how to use it when something needs fixing or when things go wrong.

Another thing that was in the notebooks, along with pictures of the floatplane, were some pictures of the graveyard. They were glued in. Some were taken when the wisteria vine was in full bloom and had those heavy purple flowers hanging all over the place.

Then there was a page where Papa had plotted out the graveyard and put everybody's name in the right place. He said he had to ask Aunt Scrap because she's the only one who knew where every grave was and who was in it.

I got Papa to put a X at the same spot where I put one on the ground with my foot—the summer me and Mark left home.

THE VINE

۶۹

The people in the graveyard were pulled together in groups. Tyree talked to a cousin, John. ". . . because that ain't what happened. What happened was they was fishing, where that overhang on Birch Creek is, and they was playing cards and Papa had been drinking Forrest Baker's whisky, more than Forrest was happy with, so when Papa said, 'Where's the red-eye?' Forrest throws it at him, under-handed, while Papa won't looking and it hit him on the chin and they got in a fight and he *bit Forrest's finger and it was always crooked. That's what happened about the finger. Forrest had been drinking with Dink while Dink's little Lia was born — little-bitty when she was born — the one they called Scrap."*

"I think you're wrong."

"Well, ask him."

"I reckon I will. Ross. Ross, how was it that. . . ."

MEREDITH

Everybody insisted the baby be named Meredith Ross Jr., and they're calling him Little Meredith, which ain't good by no stretch of the imagination. I call him Ross because that's what I can pronounce, most of the time. Some of the others are starting to call him Ross, too.

Rhonda's gone. For good, I guess.

Me and Ross and Noralee are still living with Mama and Papa. Noralee's learning a lot about babies. She's doing a good job except when she sulks.

Ross is a pistol. Looks just like me except he's got ten fingers and ten toes. He was born November the second. In October, Rhonda probably didn't say over fifteen words to me. Everybody said she was just having a hard time with the last part of the pregnancy. I typed out, "What's The Matter?" so many times I started typing out WTM and she'd just look at it and shrug her shoulders, and cry sometimes. I more or less knew what was the matter, but felt like there was some chance I might be wrong and I wanted her to talk about it, but I was getting more worked up the closer it came to baby time, and more worried, and more wondering what the hell she was going to do, and if she was going to leave before the baby was born, or after the baby was born. It was not a easy time, with me trying to learn to talk and button my shirt. And I kept remembering closer and closer up to the time when the mine exploded. We were coming into a village and Hux asked me if the road had been swept and I said it had. There was a curve in the road ahead and I saw a mangy dog on the side of the road, sitting like he was about dead. I remember seeing the curve in the road ahead, but I don't remember any blast or anything. I keep being afraid I'm going to remember it.

Mark got home three days before we left for the Christmas trip to Florida, and then he had a few days with us in Florida before he had to report back to Homestead Air Force Base in Miami. Things are going good for old Mark. He's through with the war, but he's staying in the Air Force, got him a Corvette and four or five girlfriends. Stewardesses, nurses.

I had some things I wanted to ask him and had them typed out for days before he got home. When I get to reconstructing a day or a time or an event I forget the name of something or some fact. I had forgotten the name on the tombstone we dropped down the well that time, but Mark couldn't remember it either.

We'd been up under the house dropping Mason jars down there and bombing them with rocks when we decided to put something live down there to rescue, so we stole a chicken from Mr. Gibbs's backyard—this was before Rhonda had tits

—but in the meantime we found out that Mr. and Mrs. Gibbs had a damn tombstone, a headstone thing with just the name and date, for a damn BACK DOORSTEP. They were really pretty low class. You've got to be pretty low class to have a tombstone for your back doorstep.

By that time Aunt Esther had stopped Mark from going over there except when we snuck over there, but what happened was we got more interested in dropping that tombstone doorstep down the well than in dropping the chicken down there. Somehow we figured the chicken might not work.

Or maybe we did drop that chicken down there.

Anyway, we got over there and stole that tombstone and rolled it home in the wheelbarrow—it was real heavy—and slid it up under the kitchen, leaving this swath which we brushed over like Uncle Hawk does the jeep tracks, and we propped it on the well curb like a cigarette on the edge of a ashtray and had this little ceremony where I said a speech where—

We must not have dropped that chicken down the well because I would have remembered that for sure.

Anyway, I said a speech where at the end I said this guy's name and "may he rest in peace," and that was one hell of a splash—drops of water came all the way out the top of the well.

Mark remembered that. He looked good. He'd lost a little weight, had all his arms and legs, said he'd been running three miles a day, playing handball. He's been out West at some kind of radar school before he starts learning to fly the F-4. He had two stewardesses and a nurse visit him out there. That's all he could talk about. Mark likes to talk about his women. That and the F-4. He was pretty comfortable around me. I mean he didn't give me any of this I'm-proud-of-you-and-you're-a-real-inspiration bullshit. It's damn terrible the way the human race don't know how to act around somebody that ain't the average talking Joe. Let something be a little off and people get turned on to this different frequency and they act like total assholes and don't even know it. I figured it out pretty much: Thousands of years ago they had to kill people that was screwed up, so now some of that instinct is still in the blood, and people feel guilty that they want to kill you, so they act funny.

Anyway, Mark answered some questions and talked until he ran out of things to say and didn't come back over until the morning we started out to Florida on the Christmas trip.

All the way down I knew something was bad wrong when Rhonda looked out the car window more than she looked at Ross and cried as much as he did. Mama was telling me, before Rhonda had Ross, that pregnancy affects some women that way. Then she was telling me that the first few months after the birth would be that way.

Well, what happened in Florida was that Rhonda knew these guys playing music in Key West—some of her old band —and she wanted to go down and sing, she said. She told me this on the night after the Silver Springs trip, which we always take on the second day we're there.

Rhonda and me were staying in the garage guest room because the baby would wake everybody up inside. Aunt Sybil and Uncle Hawk hadn't realized when they fixed that room up for us that there won't no way Rhonda could take care of

Ross *and* me, so Mama said she'd come out and stay with us, and Rhonda got mad as hell. Then Mama sent Noralee out there to help, and Rhonda got madder, so there was me and Rhonda and Ross in that little garage guest room the first and second night in Florida, trying to pass time.

When she told me she was leaving, she stood with her face to the wall and said, "Some of the band is in Key West playing music and I'm going to catch the bus down there tomorrow and sing with them tomorrow night . . . maybe the next night or two."

Aunt Sybil and Uncle Hawk had this crib set up in the corner and Ross was on his first shift of sleep. There was this little black-and-white TV out there, a little refrigerator, and we'd already eaten and watched TV over in the main house, and then we're out here in this room with her having just said that, and it was like feeling something fixing to explode, blow up. She was leaving me even though she chose me for better or worse, sickness or goddamned health, and I decided that I wasn't going to sit there and let her walk out on me without saying something, doing something—she was doing this to ME, leaving me alone and I hadn't done a goddamned thing. I got blowed out of the water in 'Nam. I won't about to sit there again and get blowed out of the water without doing anything. Here was somebody leaving her child and piece of a husband.

She was standing with her back to me.

I hit the wheelchair arm with my stump and stuck out my tongue as far as I could. She didn't turn around. I hit the chair again and again and again, harder and harder and harder, with my tongue out as far as I could get it—the working half of my face as ugly as I could make it. I was hitting it so hard the chair was rolling backward on the left, about a inch every hit, turning me away from her. I kept my face toward her with my tongue out while the chair turned the little bit on each hit. My rolled-up sleeve came loose and hung down. She finally turned around, ran over to me and grabbed my shoulders and screamed in my face, "Stop it! Stop it! You goddamn piece-of-nothing. Stop it!"

I kept my tongue out as far as it would go. She was goddamned free to go. I was glad of it—but not without her hearing from me first. She went over and started unpacking my suitcase which she hadn't done the night before. She put my clothes in the two bottom drawers to the dresser. She didn't hang anything in the closet and she didn't fold anything up. She just threw it all in there, mixed up. She didn't sort the underwear or socks or anything.

Hell, if I could have, I would have left, right then—with Ross.

Then she turned out the lights and there won't nothing but the light from the TV. I'm sitting in the wheelchair, glad for once that I couldn't talk because it was all a great dark cloud and I couldn't do nothing with words. My neck was hot. All I wanted to say was "Do what you have to do. Good riddance."

"I got to do it, Meredith. Esther, and Mildred, and Noralee, and Bliss can take care of Ross. That's all they do anyway. It's just one big happy family that cooks, and talks about dead people, and don't never ask anybody else about their family, and if you don't *have* a family, or if you have a shitty one, you feel like shit. And I'm having real problems taking care of a two-month-old baby and a invalid war veteran. I want to sing some music, Meredith. Anybody would. I just want to sing some music. I'm entitled to it. Goddamn, *you* birth a baby and then put up with five or six in-law mamas and I don't know what all else. I just want to sing a little music with a band. That's where my life is. And it's all disappeared."

She sat down on the bed. I watched her face—a dim white color from the TV light, while her eyes looked down at her hands. I heard her voice over and over in my head saying that about invalid war veteran and then I made it say, in my head, how she used to tell me she loved me. Because Rhonda has this gravelly voice that sometimes whispers when she don't mean for it to, it's so rough. And I figured right then like I been figuring since I got back from 'Nam that if I wanted to hear it I would have to bring it up in my mind along with the other things I'd been bringing up. So I brought it up just to listen to it for a little while, while she sat on the bed and pouted and cried.

I didn't cry. I was pretty numb. I just sat there for a long time.

The next morning—the hunting morning—it was hot and raining. Dan Braddock came in the store and talked about this real estate company he was starting—wanted Thatcher to start a branch in North Carolina. He kept telling me I still had my mind, I still had my mind. I typed out: NO I DONT. YOU DONT EITHER.

I remembered how cold it had been the last Christmas I'd been there, when Bliss came out on the back steps and sat with me. So since nobody could go hunting because of the rain, we sat around in the store. Rhonda called to find out when the bus came through, Noralee and Bliss took turns with Ross, and I sat there behind my eyes, watching, the whole time Rhonda was walking out there and getting on the bus, carrying her green overnight bag. Good looking ass. It was a sad state of things to watch—that bus pulling away, but it was sad because of all that had gone on before the war. As far as *after* the war was concerned, she hadn't took to mothering real well—I don't think she ever had any example. Me and the baby was far more than she could handle. There were too many women around anyway, it seemed like to her. And rock and roll was calling. Way down in Louisiana close to New Orleans. She could sing the hell out of that song.

MARK

Bliss says somebody needs to follow Rhonda down there and talk to her one on one, and find out for sure if she is planning to come back—ever. Rhonda said she was going to stay just one night, but Bliss isn't sure, and says that if Rhonda doesn't come back, we might never again know what she is planning to do, and that they all need to know in order to figure out how to take care of Meredith and Ross when they get back to Listre.

Mother says she wants to go along with me which I know will not work because Rhonda's going to be singing in a nightclub and all that, and Mother goes to bed at nine-thirty anyway, so I try to explain all this before I leave and she finally says she won't go. She said she just wanted some free time to talk to me.

It's a long six hours from Locklear to Key West. I've driven down to Key West twice since I've been stationed in Florida. They have a celebration at sunset every night on a dock which faces west into the ocean. The party breaks up after the sun goes down. It's a wild, good-feeling time. I figure I can get a room, catch the sunset act, then find Rhonda wherever she's singing. There're not that many places with live music.

I get a room and am driving to catch the sunset when I see Rhonda walking toward the dock with two guys. They must be band members—they're wearing jackets with "The Rockets" on the back. I pull over to a fire hydrant and call out to her.

She looks at the wrong car, then sees me and walks over. Her eyes are red. Rhonda is very, very good looking. Part of it is the way she carries herself, the way she stands with one hip forward. She's blond. Then there's the milky quality of her skin, with some kind of bronze undertone or something, and she has a deep, husky voice that's straight from the movies. And she's one hell of a singer. I don't blame her, in a way, for wanting to sing.

I need to know where I can talk to her tonight and all that, maybe eat breakfast with her tomorrow before heading back —after she's had time to calm down and think about what she wants to do. And if she wants a ride back, then she can ride back with me.

"What the hell are you doing down here?" she asks. "You following me?"

"No. I just came to give you a ride back, maybe. They were all worried about you, you know, and I volunteered to drive down here. I been down here a couple of times. Nice place."

"They ain't worried about me. They're worried about Meredith and Ross. You know that. Man, it was like I was tied in a straight jacket. I can't—" She starts crying.

"Why don't you get in and I'll take you wherever you're going, unless you're with those guys."

"I ain't with those guys. They're just in the band. We had a great gig last night—at Sloppy Joe's."

She waves bye to the guys waiting, walks around the car and gets in. Her hair is pulled up on top of her head and these little ringlets hang down on the sides. She gets in and pulls out a joint. "You ever smoked one of these?"

"Yeah." I don't tell her only one.

I start thinking, and I try to stop thinking what I am thinking, but I figure I'll just wait and see how things go. Rhonda's been stuck in a very bad situation for several months, actually over a year. And she's a sensuous woman. And we're both in Key West alone, and if she says she's not going back, I'll call Bliss, and if Rhonda really needs me in a bad way, then what the hell am I supposed to do? It's all a matter of physical geography. I mean, if I'm thinking it, and she's thinking it, *that's* the *sin*, as they say. Why the hell deprive yourself, and in this case, nobody gets hurt. That's the real situation. Nobody is getting hurt. That's more obvious than anything.

MEREDITH

Bliss went into the guest room the afternoon that Rhonda left and hung up my clothes and made up the bed and straightened things out. Ross stayed in the house with Mama that night. Thatcher rolled me out to the guest room and helped me get in bed. At different times, different people put me to bed, and if Old Blue flops out of my underwear when it's Bliss's turn, she says, "We're all family."

Ross was doing good. It's not hard for him to be kept clean and happy when Noralee, Mama, Aunt Esther, and Bliss are all looking after him. They put him in my lap for a good bit of the time and he smiles at me. I get Bliss to hang a rattle from my stump—safety-pin it to my sleeve—and I can play with him as good as anybody, especially if I'm on the floor.

At about nine o'clock on the second night, Mark called Bliss from Key West. I was in my spot at the end of the counter in the store when she took the call down at the other end. They talked for all of a minute and Bliss says to me, "Come on, let me roll you out to the guest house."

On the way over we met Thatcher. He stopped and stood while Bliss rolled me toward him.

"Sorry, Meredith," he said. "I was on the phone line. But maybe it'll be a little more relaxed without her around."

Sure, Thatcher.

When Bliss rolled me into the guest room I thought about killing myself somehow, but when she turned on the light, I saw Ross's striped T-shirt on the bed—and Bliss had her hand on the back of my neck—and I knew it won't no more than a thought.

She walked over and sat down on the bed. "Rhonda's not coming back."

I nodded.

Bliss talked about how everybody would help, that she was sure I could come live with her and Thatcher if I wanted to, that when I learned to walk and got the arm I'm supposed to get, things would get better. She didn't know I was just getting lower and lower. I felt like I was at the bottom of the barrel, end of my rope, end of the line. I didn't even have the energy to hold my mouth closed. I nodded toward the bed.

She rolled me over to the bed, clicked out the brace, stood me up in the walker, took off my coat, unbuttoned my shirt, pulled it off, unbuckled my belt, unzipped my pants and when she started pulling them down over my hips I got a hard-on. She moved the walker, held my arm, pulled back the covers, helped me sit on the bed and then lie down. She covered me up, turned me over to face the wall, walked over to the door, turned out the light, stood there a minute, then left. In a few seconds she came back in, closed the door, locked it. She took off her coat—I could hear her, my good ear was up—and got into bed behind me. She was wearing a silk-feeling blouse. She put her top arm under mine, her hand on my chest and squeezed. God, oh God, I needed it. I needed that. She massaged my chest, then my stomach, then the back of my head with her other hand; then she worked my shorts down. It was a little cumbersome. I was ready to come if she touched me, I knew. She got her other hand under my waist and found me with both her hands at the same time and began to move them first very, very slowly. . . . It was like heaven.

1971

BLISS

The splendor of the wisteria has not abated one iota.

This summer's gravecleaning group was small but proud. Aunt Scrap was there, bless her heart, with her powerful presence and her walker, which meant two walkers in all, since Meredith likes to have his along so he can stand for awhile and maybe move a few feet. He's decided not to order an electric wheelchair because he believes he'll be walking before too long. I'm not sure, but I'm hoping. His progress has been remarkable. He tried an artificial arm and leg and gave up on both. What he has been through would have killed a lesser human being for sure, but he's charged back from the abyss and is now able to clearly say some single words, and move very slowly from one spot to another by leaning over in the walker, putting his weight on his right elbow, steadying the walker with his short left arm and skipping forward with his right leg, then lifting the walker with his stub and moving it forward.

Throughout his ordeal, from the day he got back, I have seen the old Meredith in his eyes, and now when he says one word I can usually read the rest of the sentence in his eyes, which move on beyond what he's saying.

Taylor loves him because Meredith buys him something out of every government check he gets, the last thing being a baseball glove, and too, Meredith points his stump at Taylor and wiggles it and Taylor thinks it's the most mysterious and unusual thing in the world. Where the skin is sewed over the end makes a little X.

Ross was along on the gravecleaning, rolling in the truck bed on several blankets. He crawls and rolls all over the place and can pull up, but he's not big enough to fall out yet. Next year he will be. He's a sweet pretty, as Aunt Scrap would say, and looks exactly like Meredith's baby pictures. He and Meredith both are living with Thatcher, Taylor, and me. It works out because Taylor and Ross have one bedroom, Meredith the other, and Thatcher and me the other. Noralee had rather babysit than eat, so she keeps one or both of the boys over at Mr. Copeland's—enough to give me genuine relief. She helps with Meredith, too, and enjoys it, except for an occasional frustration.

Nobody made it up from Florida for the gravecleaning this year because Uncle Hawk had complications with his cataract operation. And Thatcher couldn't be there at first because he was busy at Strong Pull, where his job is taking on more and more of an administrative cast.

So the only ones there to start with were me, Meredith, Mildred, Mr. Copeland, Aunt Scrap, Taylor, Ross, and Noralee.

Mr. Copeland had come over late Friday afternoon, the day before, got Thatcher, and they went to the graveyard and did some work. Mr. Copeland knew there was going to be only a small crowd the next day, so he wanted to get some of the work done. Very early the next morning, Saturday, he went back by himself, and so it turned out that a good bit was already done when the rest of us got there.

What happened was that it turned into one of those days when the sun is bright and warm but the air is cool, and thin. It set Aunt Scrap off to talking about how there used to be more days like that around the turn of the century when she was a little girl and lived just down the road from the very spot upon which we sat.

"I guess I was about eight or ten when Tyree and Loretta started having all their children: Little Hawk, Albert, Esther, Henry, Content, Spruce, Lucy. That the right order, Albert?"

"That's right."

"I won't but three or four houses down the road, and for some reason, Papa and Mama didn't have but two of us, so I spent all the time I could at Tyree's.

"And then of course the typhoid of 1911. You ought to know about some of this," she said to Taylor, who is nine now. "You too," she said to Noralee.

"I know a lot of it," said Noralee. "I knew about the typhoid."

Aunt Scrap spat. "I remember walking in and seeing Aunt Loretta, pregnant, boiling water for Tyree, and Grandma Caroline trying to help out, refusing to take to bed, getting sicker and sicker herself, and Helen standing around wringing her hands, and Ross sitting on the porch. You know, Loretta's the one finally threw away those baby fingers that used to sit behind the clock, and it won't long after that that the fever came through.

"Son, go shoo that dog off there.

"Lord, Tyree and Grandma Caroline both died. Typhoid. And then within six weeks, those two lovely children, Henry and Content. That was Loretta losing a husband and two children within six weeks. And Ross, his mama and a son. That was a busy spring and summer in this little graveyard. Don't you know. There was Tyree dying, while all the time Grandma Caroline was giving him skunk cabbage and finally his tongue turned black and he broke out in purple spots and all the time stuck under four or five quilts sweating like nobody's business. And then Grandma Caroline gone herself within a couple of weeks.

"It was happening all through here. People dying like flies.

"Will somebody do something about that dog?"

Noralee got Rex by the collar and pulled him away from a grave.

Aunt Scrap started in again. "Then within two years Loretta married that Rogers fellow and they were all off to town. I stayed with the children the day Loretta married old man Rogers and I remember little Lucy saying something about them getting married and I asked her if she knew what getting married was and she said, 'Laying down together and getting dirt throwed over you.'

"Lord a mercy, and then in two years they were back from town with the cow. Had to leave old man Rogers to his preaching. Aunt Loretta got sucked in by him being a preacher —her so straight-laced and all."

"I remember that cow," said Mr. Copeland. "People came

from all over the place to see it—in town, I mean."

I had heard all of this many times but it never failed to interest me greatly, because my parents were born twenty years later than Thatcher's parents and these stories of child labor laws and tent preaching and a cow in town were so enticing, so authentic, and it is a major part of Taylor's heritage. He was listening attentively to the part about how they left town in a caravan with the cow, and moved back here to the old homeplace which was being rented by a family of Indians who were then allowed to live in the kitchen until they found somewhere else to live.

Then Aunt Scrap leaned over, and looked around at all of us. "I'll tell you something about Hawk you all ain't ever heard. Since he ain't here, I'll talk about him. You know he worked for a while down at Lowrey's store—about a year, I suppose. Well the fact is, he was taking things, and you know, I don't reckon I ever told this, you know, he stole me a dress out of that store. A pretty blue dress. Color of the sky. You remember that, Esther?"

"No, can't say as I do."

"Well, it's true."

"It was Albert working down there, won't it?" said Aunt Esther. "Won't it you, Albert?"

"No, it was Scrap."

"No, it was Hawk," said Aunt Scrap. "He gave me that dress and I didn't pay him nothing, and he stole one for Cousin Teresa because she took a suitcase down there one day and he filled it up in a back room and made her walk out the door with it."

"Cousin Teresa?" asked Mr. Copeland.

"Yeah, little Cousin Teresa."

"She won't old enough, was she?"

"Yes, she was."

"Why don't you tell some nice stories?" asked Miss Esther.

"I like ugly ones," said Noralee. "Nobody ever tells any of those."

"I'll tell you a ugly one," said Mr. Copeland. "Esther, you remember Hawk telling us about where babies come from?"

"Yes, I remember."

"We all *thought* they came from a stump—stump in the swamp."

Mildred was tending her fingernails and looking up every once in a while, listening. She looked over at me. We have wondered together about some of the beliefs and customs that formed this family.

"Then Hawk got us together," said Mr. Copeland, "under the sycamore tree—sitting on the root over there—me and Esther, and told us that a baby started growing in a woman's stomach after a man peed in her mouth, and nine months later the baby came out her asshole."

"Albert!" said Mildred.

"Don't be telling that," said Esther.

"Well, it's true," said Albert.

"Gross," said Noralee.

"That shouldn't be repeated," said Esther.

"Lord, have mercy," said Scrap. "At least *we* thought they came out your navel."

"That *is* stupid," said Noralee.

"My mama would have slapped your face for saying that," said Mr. Copeland.

"She slapped your face more than once," said Aunt Scrap. "She did, I guess."

"It won't stupid," said Esther. "People didn't talk about those kinds of things back then. Nobody told us about anything."

"Some people talked about sex and stuff, I'll bet," said Noralee. "Just y'all didn't."

"Let's eat," said Esther.

THATCHER

I got to the graveyard while everybody was eating. Papa told me that after the picnic we'd load up the floatplane and take it to the lake for a water run. He's had it ready for a month, but wanted to wait until Uncle Hawk was up, but Uncle Hawk couldn't come because of complications from his cataract operation. Papa says we can put Meredith in the plane and zip him around. I said sure.

We got back and loaded it out of the shop where it's been sitting in there on two tables like a red kite-bird-doghouse with two yellow wood propellers stuck on these two new aluminum engines which you still have to start in this modern day and age with, believe it or not, a lawnmower crank rope.

It ended up the ones going were me, Papa, Meredith, Bliss, Noralee, and Taylor. Taylor's finally got to be a pretty able-bodied little man.

We lifted the floatplane up off the tables, its wings folded back, and toted it around chairs, little ladders, saw, drill, hammers, pliers, and all that crap—out of the shop and set it down on the boat trailer which Papa has re-modified so the floatplane fits better. (One time a folded-back wing come loose while he was pulling it behind the truck, swung forward, and locked in the forward position, and the whole thing almost took off—the best luck he's had getting it in the air. I told him he ought to be flying it off the trailer instead of off the lake.) Then we snapped the trailer tow-wire on at the nose and strapped a long strap across it. Noralee and Taylor just painted her with a new coat of red paint and wrote on the side for her name: *Natural Suspension*. That was Meredith's idea. He typed it out on his typewriter. He couldn't say it. He still can't say much.

The way the floatplane is set up now is it's got a pontoon out from each side of the fuselage to keep it from sinking so deep, and the wingtips have little boats hung below them in case they dip in the water.

Me, Papa, and Bliss rode together in the truck cab, pulling the floatplane, and Noralee, Taylor, and Meredith rode in the truck bed.

We pulled through the upper parking lot at the lake and drove on down to the lower parking lot, which is next to the boat ramp.

When we stopped next to the boat ramp, people started gathering around to stare. Papa tells me to spread the wings. The reason he does that is so people will know what it is. He starts getting in his waders, which he don't need because of how warm it is. But he always wears them no matter what, so he can walk around in the water beside the floatplane and not get wet. While he's sitting in the front seat of the truck getting his waders on, some guy walks up and asks him if he's going to fly it, and Papa says, "She flies whenever she takes a notion." Then he says to me, "Go pay the ramp fee. We'll get Meredith out."

When I come out of the dock house and start back toward the ramp, they've unhooked the boat trailer, rolled Meredith down out of the truck bed on his two special planks, and parked him beside the truck—driver's side—on the ramp, facing uphill.

Papa is pulling the boat trailer and floatplane back up to the truck and Taylor is in the truck getting out the life preservers. Bliss and Noralee are walking toward the dock.

I'm walking along toward them, and all of a sudden Meredith starts quietly rolling backwards—his brakes popped loose, I guess—right down the ramp, and nobody sees him but me. Or hears him—we keep them wheels well oiled.

I start running and hollering. Meredith sort of looks over his shoulder in the direction he's headed, as he rolls on past the floatplane, gaining speed right on down into the water, sending out little waves, and keeps right on rolling deeper and deeper—strapped into that wheelchair.

Everybody looks at me—I'm hollering and pointing and starting to run—and then at Meredith. Bliss and Noralee start running toward him. Meredith is rolling deeper and deeper into the water, with water up around his knees and then waist and then shoulders. Papa gets the boat trailer back on the hitch so the floatplane won't roll in on top of Meredith, I guess. Meredith reaches sand or something at the end of the boat ramp, because he stops, with his chin in the water—a single, solitary head on the water.

We all splash in the water after him.

"Get behind him," says Papa, as he turns and starts *back* toward the floatplane for some reason. We got to Meredith— he looked scared and was breathing fast. We started rolling him out. Here comes Papa with the *tow-wire* from the boat trailer. He was planning to hook it to the front of the wheel-chair, I guess, but the wire was too short. He stood there holding the hook while we rolled Meredith past him and on up onto the ramp.

"Did you bring a bathing suit and towel, Thatcher?" Papa asks.

"Yessir." I decided not to say nothing about him standing there holding that tow-wire.

"Roll him over to the bathhouse, put on your bathing suit, take them wet clothes off him, dry him up, and dress him in your clothes."

"But, Papa, I—"

"Now! Me and Bliss'll get this thing in the water. Go ahead."

In a few minutes, I rolled Meredith back, all dressed in my dry clothes.

"Let's get him in there," said Papa to nobody in general, pointing to the floatplane, "for a little ride on the water. Go get them football helmets out of the truck, Thatcher."

ɜ◖

". . . and I wish I could say or even think what it was like to fly in the floatplane for the first time," said Meredith. "There wasn't a thing over my head but the sky. I could look down over the edge, which was right there at my elbow. The wind was cool and the sun hot at the same time.

"Papa seemed like he knew what he was doing. He was so happy he was red—with a smile on his face that he didn't have any control over. He was scared in his eyes, until he got the hang of it.

"We were just going for a little ride on the water and that thing started flying—lifted right up, clean and smooth away from the water. We flew out over town, over the house, and then looked down at the graveyard, here.

"Papa flew it back to the lake and made a big, wide turn, dropping down lower and lower, straightened her out and touched down into the wind. Bliss said just perfect, like a swan."

CPSIA information can be obtained
at www.ICGtesting.com
Printed in the USA
FFOW03n0952040617
36027FF